What the critics are saying...

೩೦

Wildfire

USA Today Bestselling Author

Cheyenne McCray

ELLORA'S CAVE
ROMANTICA PUBLISHING

An Ellora's Cave Romantica Publication

www.ellorascave.com

Wildfire

ISBN 1843607506
ALL RIGHTS RESERVED.
Wildfire Copyright © 2003 Cheyenne McCray
Edited by Ann Richardson
Cover art by Darrell King

Excerpt from *Wildcat* Copyright © Cheyenne McCray, 2003
Excerpt from *East of Easy* Copyright © Linda Bleser, 2006

Warning:

The following material contains graphic sexual content meant for mature readers. This story has been rated E–rotic by a minimum of three independent reviewers.

Ellora's Cave Publishing offers three levels of Romantica™ reading entertainment: S (S-ensuous), E (E-rotic), and X (X-treme).

S-*ensuous* love scenes are explicit and leave nothing to the imagination.

E-*rotic* love scenes are explicit, leave nothing to the imagination, and are high in volume per the overall word count. In addition, some E-rated titles might contain fantasy material that some readers find objectionable, such as bondage, submission, same sex encounters, forced seductions, and so forth. E-rated titles are the most graphic titles we carry; it is common, for instance, for an author to use words such as "fucking", "cock", "pussy", and such within their work of literature.

X-*treme* titles differ from E-rated titles only in plot premise and storyline execution. Unlike E-rated titles, stories designated with the letter X tend to contain controversial subject matter not for the faint of heart.

Also by Cheyenne McCray

ॐ

WILDFIRE

ॐ

Dedication

∾

To Mop and Pop
Whatever you do, don't turn the page! ;-)

Acknowledgment:

∾

Many thanks to Annie Windsor,
Nelissa Donovan and Jordan Summers
for everything you do.

Chapter One

ဢ

Dean MacLeod shifted in her saddle to alleviate the ache between her thighs as she watched her ranch hands count the cattle they'd rounded up over the weekend. While she inhaled the familiar smells of dust, livestock, and testosterone, she couldn't help but enjoy watching the men work. The flex of muscle, lean bodies in tight Wrangler jeans, leather chaps, tanned forearms…

Yummy.

The ache intensified and she shifted again, rubbing her jean-clad crotch over the leather of her saddle. Her panties were drenched and her nipples jutted out beneath her denim shirt. God did it ever turn her on to watch cowboys at work, and she just happened to employ the best looking wranglers in all of Arizona.

The air was filled with the busy hum of deep male voices and the low of cattle. Saddle leather creaked as she leaned down and rubbed her mare's neck, wondering what the men would think if she cried out with an orgasm right here by the corral. Considering that behind her back she was known as "Dean the Ice Queen," those cowboys might just tumble out of their saddles if they had any idea how erotic her thoughts were.

Damn but she needed a man. Only she'd yet to find one worth keeping.

Not since Jake Reynolds.

She frowned and straightened in her saddle. Why in the hell was she thinking about him after all these years? She was definitely over that man ages ago.

Pushing up the brim of her straw Resistol, Dean's gaze followed Jess Lawless, her new foreman. Now there was one fine looking male specimen—luscious dark brown hair, wicked blue eyes and a body that was made for sex.

In the past month since she'd hired him, she'd considered breaking her own no-dating-employees-rule when it came to Jess, and she had the impression he'd be more than happy to take her up on it. But she also knew better than to complicate things by getting involved. She never intended to get serious about anyone ever again, so why complicate a perfectly good business relationship?

Of course there was always Kev Grand, who owned the Bar One, the ranch neighboring hers. For years the man had made it clear he wanted her. She'd dated him a few times recently, but when he'd tried to do more than kiss her, she'd put him off. Mustached, blonde and hazel-eyed, he was a handsome man, but she just never felt that sizzle with him like she had with Jake.

Dammit. She had to get over the idiot. Ten years was too long to have that man come into her mind and trample all over her libido.

Sweat trickled between her breasts and she unfastened another snap on her shirt, hoping a light wind would kick up and cool her skin. September sunshine warmed her face, the sky an achingly clear blue. Not even a breeze stirred the mesquite bushes and tumbleweeds on her ranch.

September. A strange sensation came over her as her thoughts turned to another September—ten years ago, when she'd met Jake Reynolds.

Her hand automatically moved to her throat and she closed her eyes as a memory came to her, sharp and vivid.

The sound of his deep voice calling her Dee, rather than Dean like everyone else did. His sinful grin, his muscled chest and athletic thighs. And the feel of his huge cock as he slid inside her—

"Dean?"

She snapped her eyes open, a rush of heat engulfing her as she looked into Jess's blue gaze. He was sitting astride his mare. His face was coated with dirt and sweat, and damn if that didn't make him look even sexier.

With his forefinger he pushed up the brim of his Stetson, his handsome face creased into a frown. "You all right, boss?"

"You know it." She pulled her shirt away from her chest, trying to cool off, and pretended not to notice how his gaze drifted to her cleavage. "Where do we stand with the count?"

"Thieving bastards." Jess's jaw tightened and his features hardened. "We're down fifty head."

"*Fifty*?" She rolled her eyes skyward, unable to believe what he'd just said. "How the hell did they steal so many without us catching them?"

Jess's gaze had a predatory gleam before he tugged his mare's reins and turned back toward the corral. "I don't know," he said over his shoulder, "but I aim to find out."

With a groan of frustrations, Dean guided Shadow across the rangeland and to the ranch house to take a quick bath. So much for feeling horny. Jess's news was a cold shower on her arousal, giving her more important things to think about than getting laid.

* * * * *

It was a road he hadn't traveled for almost ten years, Jake Reynolds realized as his truck hit a pothole, jarring his teeth along with his memories.

Sunshine glinted off the windshield, endless acres of grass and barbwire fence scrolling by as he guided the truck down the dirt road to the MacLeod ranch. One of the largest ranches in the county, the Flying M was ten miles outside Douglas, a dingy town along the Mexico border in southeastern Arizona.

September. It had been September when he'd first met Dean MacLeod. And then he'd gone and left her six months later.

Jake's truck shimmied along the dirt road, but he barely noticed as his thoughts turned to Dee—her smile that had held all the innocence of youth and all the promise of Eve. Her seductive eyes, an unusual color of green, the same shade as her August birthstone. Her auburn hair and the tantalizing mole above her left breast. And God, those legs. Long legs she'd clamped around his hips, and her sensual cries as he buried himself inside her.

Damn. His cock had grown hard just thinking about her.

Jake gritted his teeth as he thought about the girl—the woman—he'd walked away from all those years ago. She'd been nineteen, starting her first year of college, and he'd been twenty-two, a deputy with the county sheriff's department. She'd been so young, so vibrant. And he'd nearly crushed her heart, leaving her like he did.

But at the time he thought he'd done the right thing when he'd told her goodbye. That she'd been too young. *He'd* been too young.

Being bad at long-term relationships was in his genes— at least that's what he'd thought back then. His parents had divorced when he was a teenager. Even his brother Nick's marriage had lasted less than a year, and he had always been the stable one in the family.

When Dee had told Jake that she loved him, when she started talking about raising a family, it had scared the hell out of him. He told her he wasn't ready for that kind of responsibility and it would be best if they called it quits. And he'd turned around and walked out of her life.

She was probably married now with a couple of rugrats and living off in a city in some other state. As his truck neared the MacLeod Ranch, Jake tried to comfort himself by imagining her a bit wider in the hips with bags under her eyes, and maybe a few strands of gray from chasing her kids around.

Who was he kidding? She'd still look great.

When Jake had made the decision to transfer to Douglas to be closer to his ailing mother, a part of him had hoped Dee would still be here. That they could pick up where they'd left off.

He slowed the truck as he crossed over the cattle guard that rattled and thrummed under the wheels of his 4 x 4. Herds of sleek Black Angus lined each side of the road, lifting their heads to watch him pass by and then returning to graze.

Apparently the rains had been good that summer, as the grass was still green in patches, and plentiful. He noted the well-kept barbwire fences, stock tanks and windmill. Ron MacLeod always did keep his place in fine shape, and he certainly had the money to do it.

Jake didn't expect his gut to clench the way it did when he drove up to the sprawling ranch house. A vivid memory of Dee came to him. Of her running from the front porch to greet him, her smile brilliant, throwing her arms around his neck and treating him to her soft lips. Her husky voice telling him she missed him, and her firm body pressed tight to his.

With a groan, he brought the truck to a halt in front of the MacLeod residence, dust swirling around his vehicle in a beige cloud. He took in the changes of the last ten years. The oak trees and weeping willows were taller and the porch that ran the length of the house was practically overflowing with houseplants—a woman's touch.

Had Ron gone and remarried? After Nancy MacLeod's death, everyone was sure Ron would never tie the knot again.

Jake's gaze passed beyond the house, extensive barn, corrals and ranch buildings, to the tawny mountains rising behind. The old tire swing still hung from the lower branch of the oak in front of the barn. He remembered pushing Dee in that tire, spinning it around, and claiming a kiss when he caught her to him.

Jake crammed his black Stetson on his head, climbed out of the truck and slammed the door a little too hard. Shoving the memories to the back of his mind, he headed up the steps then through the maze of plants on the porch. Wind chimes hanging from the porch's beams made a haunting sound as a breeze stirred. Almost ghostly.

But the only ghosts around were the memories of Dee. He knocked. No answer. Ron must be off working on horseback or in his truck. Jake was about to leave his card in the door when he heard a shriek.

Hair prickled at the base of his neck and he automatically grabbed his gun from the holster at his back. The scream had come from the barn. Jake made sure everything was clear and hurried to the barn, his boots making no sound as he crossed the hard packed earth.

Everything was quiet. Too quiet.

Pausing beside the open barn door, he listened, his heart beating a rapid rhythm.

"You little—" a woman said, and then a thump and another cry.

He rounded the doorway, his weapon raised. Dee MacLeod was sprawled on the barn floor with her back against a hay bale, her blouse gaping open. She was glaring into a horse stall.

Jake clenched his jaw. He'd kill the man who'd dared to lay a finger on Dee.

"Come out with your hands up!" he shouted, his eyes focused on the stall, his body crouched and prepared for the slightest movement. "Nice and slow and no one'll get hurt."

He heard a noise from Dee that he thought was a sob, and then he realized it was laughter. He allowed himself a glance in her direction and saw Dee shaking her head and giggling.

"What the hell's going on?" he muttered, not relaxing his stance.

"Go ahead, arrest the little S.O.B." Dee waved toward the stall. "Cuff him while you're at it. Once you've frisked the bugger, that is. I'll get a kick out of seeing you try."

He eased closer to the open stall and peered over the side rail to find a black calf straining against a rope tie. The corner of Jake's mouth twitched as Dee snickered behind him.

"I'm gonna have to take you in, son," he said with mock seriousness to the fire-eyed calf. "For disturbing the peace and knocking around a beautiful woman."

The moment the last two words were out of his mouth, Dee's laughter died. Jake turned to look at her, and he could see reality sinking in. Recognition dawning on her pretty face, changing her smile to a small frown.

Now, she knew. After all these years and that awful goodbye, Jake had come back to Douglas. Hurt, pride and anger flashed across her face, and then worse — an expression of indifference.

He holstered his gun then extended his hand in an offer to help Dee to her feet. She moved her fingers to her neck, seeming unable to decide if she should ignore his hand, or accept it.

He'd forgotten that nervous habit of hers. How she'd rub the base of her throat when she was feeling self-conscious or uneasy, leaving the fair skin red. And how he'd loved to kiss that soft skin whenever she did that.

As though she could hear his thoughts, she moved her fingers away from her throat. With a little tilt of her chin, she reached up and clasped his hand.

That touch, that simple touch, brought back every bit of yearning he'd ever had for her, and even when she was standing, he couldn't let go. She was tall, only four inches shorter than his six feet two. The perfect height for kissing.

And God, she still smelled the same — of the wind after a summer storm and orange blossoms, the scent that always drove him wild. Memories flowed through him — of how she had explored every part of his body with her inquisitive fingers, her sexy mouth, her sweet tongue.

"Dee." Jake's voice was husky with longing.

"It's Dean, not Dee." She jerked her hand from his and dusted off the seat of her jeans, never taking her eyes from his.

"Ah, sure." Jake's gaze dropped to the rise and fall of her chest, and his throat went dry. Dee's open denim shirt exposed the swell of her breasts and taut nipples beneath a peach satin bra. Satin that he knew could be no softer than the satin of her breasts. Breasts that he wanted to caress. Nipples he wanted to taste, right there in the barn.

"You might want to fix that." He gestured toward her shirt, holding himself back from attempting to snap it up himself. Or rather, rip the rest of the snaps open and take her right here in the barn.

Pink touched Dee's cheeks as she glanced down and then snapped her shirt closed. He took the opportunity to study her long legs in snug jeans, her auburn hair escaping the single braid that fell across her shoulder as she bent over. When she finished, she lifted her head and her green eyes met his.

"It's been a long time," Jake said softly.

"Yes. It has." Frowning, Dee took a step forward, and to his surprise she reached out her hand and touched the scar that creased his left cheek. Just that slight contact was enough to make him hard in a hurry. "What happened?"

Jake shrugged. "Drug bust that went down a little wild."

"A little more than wild, I'd say." Her finger trailed the scar that went from his ear almost to his mouth. She paused, her gaze riveted on his lips, and he all but stopped breathing.

Dee jerked her hand away and took a step back, her cheeks going pink again. "So. What are you doing here?"

I came back for you. Likely Dee wouldn't be too keen on him telling her he'd come back for her ten years after he left. Instead, he took a deep breath and said, "Is your dad around?"

A glimmer of laughter came back into her eyes. "If he was, he'd likely run you off with his old Remington."

"I was afraid of that." Jake's mouth turned up in a self-deprecating grin, and then his tone went serious. "I've missed you."

She cocked her head and studied him for a moment. "Did you have anything in particular to say to my dad, or something you can tell me?"

Jake fished his wallet out of the back pocket of his Wranglers, drew out his business card and handed it to her.

Dee took it from him, her fingertips lightly brushing his, and glanced at the card. "So, you're now a Special Agent with Customs."

"I transferred to Douglas last week," he said as he slid his wallet into his back pocket. "I'm out introducing myself to ranchers in the area. The mountains behind your ranch are being used to smuggle narcotics from Mexico."

"What's new? That's been going on for years." Dee shrugged. "Enough drugs and illegals come through that range to keep every cop in the U.S. busy."

Jake frowned. True, it was common knowledge, but it still bothered him that Dee seemed so unconcerned that danger was at her back door. "If you see anything suspicious, give me a call."

She fixed a smile on her face as she shoved the card into the front pocket of her jeans. "Great, Agent Reynolds."

"Agent Reynolds?" He shook his head. "I was kinda hoping I'd still be just Jake to you, Dee."

"Dean, not Dee." She folded her arms beneath her breasts. "So that's why you came back?"

"I requested the transfer." He shrugged. "My mom's not doing so good."

Dee's features softened into concern. "Is she okay?"

"She's pretty much housebound, and she's lonely as hell." Jake scowled at himself. "I shouldn't have stayed away for so long."

And I should never have left you.

A black horse whickered and poked its head over a stall door, and Dee moved toward it. "How's my boy?" she murmured as she rubbed the horse's muzzle.

She stood in a shaft of sunlight and Jake's breath caught in his throat. Dust motes swirled in the air around Dee, and her hair shone like burnished copper.

"How's your brother doing?" she asked, her attention on the horse.

Jake swallowed, wishing Dee was stroking him instead of the damn horse. "Nick's with the county Sheriff's Department. What's your sister up to?"

"Trace got a wild hair after she graduated from college and she's been in Europe ever since." Dee rubbed the horse behind his ears. "Sometime before Christmas she'll be coming home. First visit in four years."

Jake gave a low whistle. "That's a long time to be gone from home."

"You should know." Dee patted the horse's neck and turned back to Jake. "I heard you were stationed along the Texas border."

"From the time I graduated from the academy." He moved closer, wanting to be near her. "How about you? What've you been up to all this time?"

Dee flicked a piece of straw off the top of the stall. "Other than trying to figure out who swiped fifty head of cattle, not a whole hell of a lot."

"Rustlers?"

"Yeah." She grimaced. "Week before last it started. A dozen or so heifers just up and missing. But now it looks like the bastards are getting cockier."

His mouth tightened. "Or stupider."

With a sigh that made her frustration clear, she leaned back and braced her arms on the stall behind her. The motion caused her breasts to jut out and her blouse to gape, showing that satin bra and her generous cleavage.

Jake swallowed. Hard. "When'll your dad be back?"

"He was here a week ago, so he's not likely to visit for at least a couple of months. We expect him and his new wife for Thanksgiving or Christmas, not sure which."

We. Shock rippled through Jake as it occurred to him that Dee truly could be married, living at the ranch with her husband. No ring on her finger, but that didn't mean anything. She could keep it off while she was working. He'd thought he was prepared for the possibility, but right now he couldn't imagine any man being with her.

Jake had been her first lover, and he should have been her only lover.

No, damn it. He'd given up that right the moment he walked away.

He rubbed the scar on his cheek. "Ron retired?"

"Couple of years ago." Dee nodded as she spoke, moving her arms across her chest again, as though protecting herself from Jake.

"So, you and your, ah, husband, run the ranch?"

She lifted one elegant brow and the corner of her mouth raised. "No, I do."

He couldn't help it. He had to ask. "What does your husband do?"

"Not a darn thing," she replied, and at his questioning look, she laughed. "I'm not married."

Relief surged through him, hot and satisfying. "You never married?" he said softly.

That fiery glint came back in her eyes, rivaling the devil of a calf a few stalls down. "Well, I wasn't pining after you, if that's what you're asking."

He smiled. "Who'd you mean by we?"

She shrugged and returned his smile. "My Border collie, Blue."

Jake laughed and when Dee spoke again, her voice was low. "What about you? Did you ever marry?"

"Who'd marry this ugly mug?"

She cut him a sharp glance. "If you're fishing for a compliment, you've come to the wrong woman."

"Then I'll give you one." Jake moved a step closer. "Sweetheart, how'd you grow to be more gorgeous than you were a decade ago? You were the most beautiful thing I'd ever seen that first time I laid eyes on you at the rodeo, when I watched you win the barrel racing competition."

He sucked in his breath at the memory and shook his head. "And now...look at you."

Dee closed her eyes. "I'd forgotten how you always knew the most charming words."

Before Jake realized what he was saying, he asked, "You think it's possible to be...friends...again?"

"Friends?" She opened her eyes and moved her fingers to her throat. After a moment's hesitation, she gave him a shrug and a little smile. "Why not? We're almost ten years older and we've both grown up...a lot."

Her eyes roamed over him as she spoke the last words, and he wanted her more than ever before. And that was saying something.

When her gaze met his again, he knew she'd noticed his desire. "Yes," she said, her voice low and husky. "We're both all grown up."

In the next instant, she dodged around him and headed to the stall with the calf that looked like he must be the spawn of Satan himself. "You little imp," she crooned as she laid her hand on the upper railing of the stall. "What the hell am I going to do with you?"

The calf glared, his head lowered and looking as though he'd like to take her out, and Dee laughed. "You're going to end up at the slaughterhouse rather than becoming lord of the manor with all the pretty ladies at your beck and call, if you don't settle down."

"What's the sonofabitch's name?"

"Imp." Dee glanced over her shoulder at Jake. "I thought about naming him Jake, but that's what I named the old jackass out back." She said it with a straight face, but he saw the ornery spark in her eyes.

He chuckled and shook his head. He'd forgotten her teasing sense of humor and her ability to make him laugh. She turned back to the calf, and Jake walked up behind her so that just inches separated them. He drank in the scent of her that mingled with the smells of horse, hay, sweet oats and barn dust.

"Dee." He noticed the slight shiver that ran through her at the sound of his voice.

"I keep telling you, it's Dean." She spun around and her eyes widened when she saw how close he was. She tried to step away, but her back was against the side of the stall.

"You've always been Dee to me," he murmured.

She raised her chin, and he noticed a streak of dirt across her cheek. "It's Dean to you now, just like everyone else."

Almost without thought, Jake reached up to wipe the smudge away, needing to feel the softness of her skin beneath his fingertips. Her lips parted and her eyes widened as he gently smoothed the dirt from her cheek. Slowly he trailed his thumb down her soft skin to her full lips. Needing to touch her. Needing to wipe away the memories of their goodbye.

"It's been much too long," he murmured lost in the sensation of being near Dee again, her presence seeping into his blood like wildfire.

Dee's lips trembled beneath his thumb. In the next instant she jerked away and pushed past him, heading out the barn door, her head high. He followed, catching up to her in a few strides. She stopped by the door of his black truck, obviously intending for him to leave.

The breeze blew a strand of auburn hair across her face and she absently pushed it behind one ear. Her expression was composed, but her eyes gave her away—he'd rattled her. And he was sure he'd seen longing in their depths. She extended her hand. "Friends."

Jake took her hand in his and desire curled through his belly, burning through his soul. As she pulled her hand away he knew she wanted him to leave, but he needed to be near her a little longer. There was so much he wanted to ask her now that he'd seen her again. So much he wanted to know about her.

So much time to make up for before he claimed her for good.

Before he could get out another word, Dee said, "It was...*nice*...to see you again." She gestured toward the house. "I've got to check on Blue. If he'd been up to snuff, you probably never would've made it out of your vehicle."

Jake glanced in the direction she pointed, then back to Dee. "What's wrong with him?"

"That's the weird part." With a confused frown, Dee shook her head. "Last night I found him eating raw meat, but I'm not sure where he got it. The vet was out to see Blue a little while ago, and said it could have been poisoned meat that someone set out to kill off coyotes in the area."

Narrowing his gaze, Jake said, "You think it might have been the rustlers trying to get your dog out of the way?"

Dee's face seemed to go a shade whiter. "I did lose a lot of cattle last night, but from our eastern range. Why would they need to poison Blue?"

Jake took a step closer to Dee. "You live alone?"

She nodded as she stepped back from him. "Have been for the past few years, since my sister Trace has been in Europe."

"I don't like any of this a damn bit." Jake caught Dee by her upper arms, keeping her from retreating any farther. "You need to watch out for yourself."

"I've been doing just fine." She placed her palms to his chest and pushed him away, forcing him to break contact. "I'd better see how Blue's doing."

"You be careful." Jake tipped the brim of his Stetson then grabbed the door handle of his truck. "Later, Dee."

"Dean." She smiled too brightly. "See you around, Agent Reynolds." And with that, she strode toward the house without a backward glance.

As she jogged up the steps and crossed the porch, he watched her fluid movements. He had a side view, and couldn't help enjoying it. The way her breasts bounced and her tight backside swayed. She opened the front door and then closed it behind her.

He shook his head as he got into his truck and tossed his hat onto the seat beside him and grinned.

No matter what Dee MacLeod might think, Jake intended to make her his woman again—this time for keeps.

Chapter Two

ဢ

Jake Reynolds. His name rippled through Dean in silvery waves as she leaned against the closed door, her eyes shut, his image filling her mind.

His sinfully black hair, the hard planes of his face, the fine lines at the corners of his eyes when he smiled, and the cleft in his chin that she had loved to run her tongue over. And Lord, that muscular physique—his broad chest, lean hips and powerful thighs.

She waited until she heard his truck start. After the sound of the engine had completely faded, she rubbed her sweating palms over her jean-clad thighs and opened her eyes.

When he'd come barreling into the barn, it was as though her thoughts about him that morning had summoned him to her—and it was like he belonged there.

Jake. Jake was back.

For a moment all she'd been able to do was stare at him. So many thoughts had flashed through her mind. In that instant, she had wanted to yell at him for breaking her heart into a thousand pieces. And then she wanted to throw her arms around him and let him hold her like he used to.

How could she feel like that after the way he'd left her?

For six months they'd been virtually inseparable. Even though he'd never told her, she'd been so sure he was in love with her. One day she'd shared with him her hopes and dreams for the future, and for raising a family. She'd told Jake she loved him.

He'd gone quiet, and everything Jake uttered in the next moment had hit Dee like a hammer blow: *Not ready for that kind of commitment...both too young...best if we break it off before things get any more serious...don't want to hurt you...leaving for the academy to become a Customs Agent...*

And like that, it was over. He had run away from her and her love.

She'd had almost a decade to prepare for the off chance that she'd see Jake again. But nothing had prepared her for today. How could he look even more handsome at thirty-one than he had at twenty-two?

Back then he'd been muscular and solid, but he'd filled out in a hard, masculine way that made him sexier than ever. Even that scar made his features more rugged and heartbreaking.

And those gray eyes that shifted with his moods from liquid silver when he laughed, to dark and passionate when they had made love and he was deep within her.

"Get a grip, Dee," she muttered, and then stomped her boot on the tile. *Dammit!* She hadn't thought of herself as anything but Dean since Jake had left her all those years ago. Only Jake had ever called her Dee. To everyone else she was Dean, short for Claudine, a name she'd hated when she was growing up.

But that first night when she'd met him at the rodeo dance, Jake had shaken his head and murmured, "Sweetheart, you're too gorgeous to have a man's name." And when he called her Dee, he made her feel like the most beautiful woman on Earth.

Just like today. The sound of her name on his tongue, a husky murmur, had been a caress that stirred the fire within her and brought back wave after wave of memories.

Memories of his strong arms surrounding her, his mouth claiming hers, his hands roaming through her hair, his lips moving to the sensitive spot at the base of her throat. Memories of his cock plunging inside her as he made love to her.

No, it hadn't been making love. It was just fucking.

She sighed and brought her hand to her neck. An unbelievable, incredible fuck at that. If it had been making love, and if Jake had truly cherished her, he never would have left.

A warm flush filled her at the thought of how close they had stood to one another in the barn, inches apart, his earthy scent surrounding her, and the fact that his arousal had been as plain as day. God but his cock had looked good pressed against his tight jeans.

And that touch — she'd almost melted at the feel of his thumb against her cheek and lips. It had been all she could do to walk away from him.

Amazingly enough, she couldn't help but feel flames of passion igniting in her breasts, her belly, between her thighs. She could almost feel his large hands clasping her hips, his sensual mouth on her skin, his tongue seeking out her nipples in slow, lazy circles.

Stop it, Dee! She groaned and hit her head back against the door. *Dammit, not Dee! Dean, Dean, Dean, Dean!*

But she couldn't get thoughts of their incredible sex out of her mind. Before she even realized what she was doing, she pulled the snaps of her blouse apart and unhooked the front of her bra. Her breasts spilled out of the satin cups and onto her palms. Closing her eyes, she pulled and twisted her nipples, imagining Jake's tanned hands against the paleness of her breasts.

She moved her hands along her belly, unbuttoned her jeans and pushed them down her thighs. A moan escaped her as she slid the fingers of one hand into the curls and then into her wetness. Her other hand returned to fondle her nipples, that ached for the feel of Jake's mouth.

The image of his muscular body was clear in her mind as her fingers stroked her clit. How she had enjoyed going down on him, wrapping her lips around his cock as his hands fisted in her hair. His hoarse shout when he came and the taste of his semen as it filled her mouth.

Her breathing became more rapid as she worked her clit, picturing Jake's mouth and tongue licking her as her knees clenched his head between her thighs. And as soon as she came, he would bring her ankles around his neck and thrust inside her, fucking her harder and harder until she screamed with another orgasm.

Tension wound up inside Dee, tighter and tighter until it exploded, her climax so intense that she cried out. She continued stroking her clit as her body shuddered with wave after wave of pleasure, and then she came again.

Feeling dizzy and lightheaded, she rested against the door, trying to catch her breath.

The sound of a boot step came from the direction of the kitchen and Dee froze.

Was someone in her house?

Heart pounding, she pulled up her jeans and fixed her bra and shirt. Hair prickled at her nape as she walked to the kitchen.

Empty.

Relief flooded her — but then she noticed the slight sway of the swinging doors that led to the backroom and the garage.

Someone had been in her house.

And they'd just watched her masturbate.

A low whine caught her attention and her gaze snapped to Blue. He half-opened his eyes, his tail thumping weakly on the bedding of the nest she'd made him next to the refrigerator.

She knelt beside the Border collie and stroked his silken throat. "All right. Who'd you let in, boy? It had to be someone you know, 'cause sick or not I know you would have at least barked if it was a stranger."

"You're not talking, huh?" Dee tried to calm the racing of her heart as she talked to Blue. "Well, I'll let it slide this time since you're not feeling so good." Blue whined again and pushed his nose under her fingers, asking her to rub behind his ears the way he liked it. She sank down on the floor to give him the attention he was asking for. "Tell you what. If I find out that someone deliberately tried to poison you, I'm going to personally kick their ass."

Her thoughts turned back to the intruder in her home. Since Blue hadn't growled, she knew it had to be someone he was familiar with. And oddly enough, the thought of someone she knew watching her was kind of erotic. It had to have been one of the ranch hands—or could it have been a neighbor, like her friend Catie Wilds, or even Kev Grand? Perhaps even her foreman, Jess?

Jake's face filled her mind—it couldn't have been him, now could it? No, she would have heard his truck.

While she gently stroked Blue, she sighed, thinking about how she had touched Jake's scar and the desire that had risen up inside her like a summer thunderstorm.

Dammit! You've got to stop thinking about him.

All of a minute went by, but it was hopeless. She couldn't get her thoughts off the man. The way his cleft deepened when he grinned, the powerful lines of his body, and the smoldering sensuality. She'd need to get her vibrator out if she didn't cool down.

She was absurdly pleased that he hadn't married. Had he even come close? When she told him she hadn't been pining over him all this time, it had only been the partial truth.

True, she had gotten on with her life, but no man had ever measured up to Jake. She had often wondered if perhaps her memories had become distorted, and that he wasn't half the man she remembered him to be. But after today, she knew the truth.

He was twice the man she remembered.

Damn.

Dee put her face close to Blue's. "If you were feeling well I'd bet you'd have chased that nasty old man off our property."

The collie flicked out his pink tongue and kissed the end of Dee's nose, causing her to giggle. "I know. Next time he comes around, if there is a next time, you'll set him straight."

She sighed and rubbed at a stain on her faded jeans. Ten years later and Jake was back in town — wanting to be friends.

Friends!

A slow grin spread across her face as a devilish thought crossed her mind. She just might have to show Jake Reynolds what he'd been missing.

* * * * *

When Dee had walked into her house and shut the door behind her, it had been all Jake could do not to follow her inside. Instead, he started his truck and drove away from her ranch, his hands clenched tight around the steering wheel. As his tires rattled back over the cattle guard, he thought about how her blouse had been gaping open in the barn, her breasts straining against their satin bonds, and his cock hardened in a rush.

With a hell of a lot of effort, Jake fought down the lust that had filled him since seeing her. He forced his thoughts from the beauty and fire of Dee to the chill of having to meet an old rival. Not an enemy, but almost as bad.

The Bar One bordered the Flying M, so he didn't have far to drive. Just as he was about to pull onto the road that would take him to Grand's home, he spotted two men and a couple of horses alongside the southern fence of the ranch. Taking care not to stir up too much dust, Jake slowly pulled off the side of the dirt road and parked.

He slapped on his Stetson, climbed out of his truck and sauntered across the road to where the men were working on the fence. A late afternoon wind picked up, stirring the grass and causing dust to swirl on the road. It was the tail end of summer and still plenty warm, and would be for at least another month yet.

The men were on the other side, facing Jake. He didn't recognize the one guy—a large man in a khaki work shirt. The second man wore a western hat and his head was down, so Jake couldn't make out who he was until he looked up.

"Grand," Jake said when he recognized the owner of the Bar One.

"Reynolds." Kev Grand stood, pulled off his leather work gloves, and stuffed them into the back pocket of his jeans, along with a pair of wire cutters.

He and Jake were the same age and had gone through high school together in Douglas, but they'd never been what anyone would call friends. Their rivalry had started when Cathy Pierson chose to go to the Freshman Winter Dance with Jake instead of Kev, and went on to their senior year when Jake had been selected captain of the Douglas Bulldogs football team. They'd damn near come to blows a few times, and it was a wonder they never had.

Grand was a good two inches shorter than Jake, slimmer in build, wiry and athletic. By the way the man was eyeing him, and by the way his handlebar mustache curved down into a serious frown, Jake had the impression that Grand was none too pleased to see him, either.

Jake extended his hand through the barbwire fence to the man he didn't recognize. "Jake Reynolds."

"Ryan Forrester." The big man took Jake's hand and shook it. "Deputy with the Sheriff's Department."

"I'm sure we'll be running into one another," Jake said. "I'm with Customs." He turned to Grand. "How're you doing these days?"

Grand spit into the dirt at his feet then glanced down the road toward the MacLeod ranch and back to Jake. "What the hell are you doing back in these parts?"

Jake gave a wry smile. Not that he'd expected Grand to slap him on the back and ask him to go have a beer. But he figured the man was carrying childhood grudges a little too far.

"I'm working." Jake pulled out his card and handed it over the fence to Grand. "I'm stationed in Douglas now."

Jake studied the lines of Grand's frown as the man took the card, glanced at it and slid it into the pocket of his denim work shirt.

"Customs. Yeah." Grand nodded. "So, tell me, Reynolds. What Customs work took you out to the Flyin' M?"

Jake pushed back the brim of his Stetson and eyed Grand squarely. So that's what it was—Grand had a thing for Dee. For all Jake knew, Dee and Kev Grand could be seeing each other.

The thought of Grand and Dee fucking one another was enough to give Jake the urge to knock the living daylights out of the man. Well damned if he was going to let the bastard have her now.

Fighting back the desire to slam his fist into Grand's jaw, Jake said, "I'm working this area, so you have my number if you need anything."

Grand placed his hands on the top strand of the barbwire fence, between the barbs. His shirt was soaked with sweat at the armpits and around the collar, and a dark ring stained the crown of his hat. He flexed his fingers and narrowed his hazel eyes. "You had your chance with Dean MacLeod. Don't think you can come back and start where you left off."

Jake glanced down at his boots. He felt a muscle on his face twitch, the only outward indication that Grand's words had royally pissed him off.

Looking back at Grand, Jake fought to keep his tone even, his expression blank. "Like I said, I'm working the area."

"Uh-huh." Grand spit into the dirt again and then fixed his gaze on Jake. "Is that all you need?" The rancher gestured toward the fence. "Damn rustlers cut through and I've gotta fix it before my cattle get out."

"Reckon I'll be on my way." Jake nodded to Ryan Forrester, pulled the brim of his Stetson down and walked back to his truck.

As Jake strode away, Grand called after him, "You just remember what I said about Dean MacLeod, you hear?"

Refusing to acknowledge Grand's parting shot, Jake climbed into his truck and headed on out.

Slamming the apartment door behind him, Jake tossed his hat onto the coffee table and headed into the kitchen. It was a few hours after his talk with Kev Grand, but he was still pissed.

After looking in the bare cabinets and staring into the empty fridge, Jake realized he was going to have to do some grocery shopping or starve. To hell with that. He'd have a couple of pizzas delivered, along with an order of Buffalo wings and breadsticks. That ought to get him through dinner and breakfast.

Jake went to the sink and splashed cold water over his face. No clean dishtowels or paper towels, so he wiped his wet face on his sleeve.

The sparsely furnished apartment smelled like fresh paint and mothballs, and wasn't even close to feeling like a home. He was renting until he found a place he wanted to buy, maybe a piece of land where he could build a new house. Most of his stuff was still in storage, and the apartment had about as much appeal as a jail cell.

He had to figure out some way to get close to Dee again, to get her to let him back in her life. With a frustrated sigh, he went to the sliding glass doors and peered through the blinds. The apartments had been built close to the fairgrounds where rodeo events were held several times a year. The County Fair took up four days every September, and it was that time of year again. In the darkness he could see the glittering lights of the midway and floodlights illuminating the rodeo grounds.

That time of year. The same time of year he'd met Dee, ten years ago. And this Friday would be the rodeo dance.

He stared across his apartment at the phone and made up his mind. What was the worst that could happen? Dee could hang up, which basically put him right back where he was anyway.

Alone and fantasizing about having the woman in his bed.

Many times. Many ways.

In two determined strides, he reached the phone in the cramped living room. He shoved aside a stack of newspapers, sat on the couch, picked up the handset, and started dialing. Funny how he still remembered the MacLeod's phone number, as though he'd called Dee yesterday. Unless she'd changed the number.

The phone rang a couple of times, and then Dee's sensual voice said, "Hello?"

Damn, but just hearing her made him hard. "Hey, sweetheart."

A pause. "Jake. I—I didn't expect it to be you."

His gut tightened. Who *did* she expect?

He took a deep breath and tried to keep his voice calm. "Did you think it might be Kev Grand?"

"Kev? Why would you say that?"

"I saw him today after I stopped by your place." Jake clenched the phone so hard his knuckles ached. "He made it clear you two are together."

"*He what*?"

Jake grinned and relaxed, a little of the tension easing from his muscles. At least Dee didn't think of herself as Grand's woman, even if she might be dating the man.

"He saw me coming from your place and gave me some advice. Told me in so many words to stay away."

"Well that's taking neighborliness a little far," Dee muttered. "Is that what you called about?"

"I wanted to ask you something."

"What?"

Jake swallowed. How hard could it be? "Ah...I was wondering if you'd like to go to the rodeo dance with me this Friday."

Silence. "Are you asking me on a date?"

She wasn't going to make this easy. "Yeah, I guess I am."

A longer silence. "Why are you asking me out?"

"It'd be a start towards being friends."

What the hell was he saying?

"Friends," she repeated, her tone flat, even a little hard. "That's all you want?"

Jake rubbed his hand over his face. "It's a beginning."

"A beginning to what?"

"Will you go with me or not?"

Dee sighed and he imagined her fingers at her throat, the soft skin turning pink. "Tell you what," she finally said, "I'll be there, and I'll save a dance for you."

"One dance?" Jake leaned back against the couch and stared at the ceiling. If that was all she'd give him, he'd take it. *For now.* "All right."

"See you Friday, then," she said softly. God, but her voice was sexy. "So long, Jake."

"Bye." Jake punched off the phone and tossed it onto the couch.

Grinning, he got to his feet and headed to the bathroom to wash off the day's grime and sweat.

Once he was beneath the hot spray, he couldn't help but remember the times he and Dee had showered together. When he'd washed her hair and soaped her breasts. And while under the spray he'd knelt and licked her clit until she screamed

Moist steam clouded the bathroom as Jake soaped his own body, imaging it was Dee's hands washing him, stroking him. As he rinsed off, he took himself in hand, wrapping his fingers around his thick cock. Warm water pelted his back and he closed his eyes as he worked his shaft from base to tip and back.

Yeah, he could feel his cock sinking into Dee's pussy. While he fucked her mindless, her head would be thrown back, her copper hair splayed across his pillow, and she would be shouting at him to go harder. Faster.

Jake's body corded as he came in a rush and he barely bit back a shout. He continued milking his cock, the semen squirting onto the glass shower door until he was empty.

When he had spilled every drop, he placed both hands on either side of the shower door and let the shower spray pelt his relaxed muscles. He couldn't wait to see Dee at the dance.

She might think she was only giving him one dance, but Jake had other ideas.

Chapter Three

ဢ

Weary, but thrilled with all her purchases, Dee carried in several packages and dress bags from her Range Rover. It was dark outside and she'd just spent a long day with her best friend Catie, hitting their favorite spots at the Tucson malls, and darn near closing the stores down.

It had been good not to think about real life—failed relationships, missing cattle, the ranch's dwindling resources. Those damn rustlers were having a heyday. Thank God for nest eggs. If Dee's mother hadn't left her a sizable trust, the cattle thefts might have closed the Flying M already.

Enough. I'm not thinking about problems today, just a little sweet, hot revenge.

Having offered to help her put everything away, Catie trailed Dee into the house, arms loaded with packages, too.

Using her elbow, Dee flipped on the light to the backroom before going through the swinging doors to the kitchen. "Thanks for shopping with me."

"Anytime, girlfriend," Catie said as she followed close behind.

Dee paused by her Border collie. "Hello luv. I'd pet you but my hands are full."

Blue just thumped his tail and gave her an adoring look. If he'd been feeling well, he would have met her at the door.

Catie blew a strand of short blond hair out of her chocolate brown eyes. "Want these in the bedroom?"

"Uh-huh." Dee skirted Blue and led the way down the hall and laid her packages on a settee.

Catie grinned as she scattered her share of shopping bags across the huge bed. "When Jake sees you in that outfit tomorrow night, you're gonna make that man so horny he won't be able to walk straight."

Laughing, Dee pulled out the ivory halter dress from one of the bags and hung it in her closet. "That's the idea, Sweatpea."

"How about a margarita while you put all that crap away?"

"Sounds like the perfect end to the perfect day of shopping." Dee grinned at her friend. "You know where everything is. And make mine a triple."

"You betcha." Catie bounced from the room, humming a catchy tune.

It wasn't long before Dee heard the whir of the blender and crunch of ice as Catie fixed their frozen margaritas. While Dee slipped the new garters, stockings and thong into her underwear drawer, she couldn't help but wonder what Jake would think when he saw her in the barely-covers-anything outfit.

Catie returned and placed a frosty margarita glass into Dee's hands as she said, "God but I could use a nice relaxing bath."

Dee took a sip of the margarita. *Heaven.* "How 'bout taking a dip in the whirlpool?"

"Wonderful idea, but I don't have a bathing suit in my back pocket." Catie held a hand up before Dee could reply. "And don't bother trying to loan me one of yours. I'd be flashing my non-existent breasts in those melon holders."

Dee rolled her eyes as she took another swallow of her drink. "Yeah, right. Your tits are fine."

"How about skinny dipping?" A dare-you look brightened Catie's gamin face. "First one in gets to fuck your foreman."

Exploding with laughter, Dee said, "You're on."

They both set their margaritas down, but before Dee even had her jeans off, Catie was naked, margarita in hand, and streaking out the French doors to the private whirlpool in the enclosed backyard. By the time Dee made it to the tub, Catie had turned it on and was stepping down into the bubbling waters.

Brilliant stars were scattered across the inky sky, the moon just a sliver and hanging low above the mountains. The night air smelled of fall and of the honeysuckle blooming on the trellis along the back porch. Dee's back yard was bordered with trees and bushes, giving the whirlpool plenty of privacy, the only light coming from a few artfully appointed landscape lights.

Evening air felt cool on Dee's body, and her nipples hardened. She stepped from the redwood decking into the warm water where Catie already waited. The feel of the water rising over her skin was erotic as Dee eased onto the seat and set her drink on the decking.

Catie sighed as she reclined. The chocolate-eyed blonde had a petite, athletic figure, unlike Dee's generous curves and willowy height. Catie's breasts were small and pert, her nipples high and pouty.

"I won," Catie murmured as she relaxed against the pillowed edge of the whirlpool and took a long draught of her margarita. "I get to fuck Jess."

Dee had just taken a drink of her own margarita and almost snorted it out her nose when she giggled. "You should go for it—I bet he'd say yes and have you in bed in a hurry."

"Ha!" Catie's small breasts rose out of the water as she straightened in her seat and faced Dee. "The man doesn't know I exist."

Dee downed more of her drink. "Well, we'll just make him notice you."

"Where'd you find such a stud for a foreman, anyway?" Catie cocked her head.

"A friend of your brother's referred Jess to me when my last foreman moved to Montana." Dee positioned herself so that her legs where slightly spread and one of the jet sprays was directly on her clit. "Oh. Right there."

"Well, Steve never told me that." Catie raised an eyebrow as her gaze traveled Dee's length. "What are you doing?"

"Mmmm." Dee smiled, enjoying the feel of the stimulation. "If you catch one of the jet streams just right, it makes for one hell of a vibrator."

"All this time and you haven't been sharing?" Grinning, Catie shifted in her seat, until she was side-by-side with Dee, their bodies touching from their shoulders down to their thighs. "Ahhhh, yeah. That'll do it."

Dee felt deliciously lightheaded and oh-so-mellow. "Uh, how much tequila did you put in those margaritas?"

Catie gave a devilish grin. "Triple, like you said."

Dee took a long draught and placed her glass on the decking behind her. "You little shit."

"I know." Catie set aside her own almost-empty glass. "But doesn't it feel great?"

"Uh-huh." Dee moved so that the spray struck her higher on her clit, a warm feeling sliding through her, as she grew hornier by the second. "Are you picturing Jess, naked?" she asked as her own thoughts turned to Jake and that cock she had once enjoyed so much.

"Oooooh, yes." Catie squirmed and spread her legs farther apart, pressing against Dee's. "I've seen Jess without his shirt, and God does he ever have a bod to make you wet."

Dee turned her head and grinned at Catie. "He's probably nine inches, you think?"

Catie's eyes were dreamy as she looked at Dee. "Ten, at least." Her gaze dropped to Dee's chest, and for a moment she just stared.

Dee shifted, her nipples hard and aching. "You all right, Sweetpea?"

"Um…Dee…" Catie's voice was low and hesitant as she continued to look at Dee's chest. "Have you ever wondered what it would feel like to—to touch another woman's breasts?"

A slow heat traveled through Dee that had nothing to do with the margarita, the warm whirlpool waters or the stimulation of the jet stream on her clit. "Well…yeah. A couple of times."

"I mean I've always preferred men. God, you *know* I love men." Catie almost looked as though she was in a trance as she stared at Dee's breasts. "But I've been…curious."

Dee held her breath as Catie's hand came up, slowly, as though she wasn't sure what she was doing. But when Catie's palm cupped Dee's breast, she couldn't help but feel aroused. The sensual combination of her legs spread and the jet spray stimulating her pussy, and the soft caress of Catie's hand, was completely erotic.

Encouraged, Catie ran her fingers over the nipple, and then moved her hand to Dee's other breast. "Is this all right? Just touching?"

"It's different," Dee murmured. Catie's hands were so soft compared to a man's. "Feels good."

"What do you fantasize about when you touch yourself?"

With a small groan of pleasure, Dee replied, "Jake. The way he caressed me. The way he felt inside me."

"Are you thinking about him now?" Catie's breath was warm as her mouth neared Dee's nipple. "Are you imagining him between your legs?"

"His cock is so big." Dee widened her thighs to the jet spray. Catie flicked her tongue over Dee's nipple, and she arched her back so that she was fully in Catie's mouth. Her lips — so soft, her tongue swirling and licking. "I used to love it when he fucked me. I couldn't get enough of him."

"Mmmm." Catie sounded like she was purring. "Did he fuck you slow and easy, or hard and fast?" she asked as she rose up on her knees and moved her mouth to Dee's other breast.

"Both." Dee gripped the edge of the stone seat as the jet spray and Catie's mouth on her nipple brought her closer to climax. Catie slid her fingers between Dee's thighs, stroking her clit, and Dee gasped, her voice breathless as she continued, "But I liked it best when he was pounding into me."

"I have something to confess," Catie whispered, as she pressed closer, her vanilla musk scent surrounding Dee. "I, um…I saw you masturbating yesterday. And it really made me horny. I never thought seeing a woman do that would be such a turn-on."

"Oh." Dee's eyes widened, but then they rolled back as Catie's touch grew stronger. "I thought someone had been there," she murmured. "And it was a kind of exciting to imagine being watched."

"I'm glad." Catie's voice rose over the bubbling of the whirlpool. "Now about Jake. Did he ever bend you over and slide his cock in you from behind?"

"Mmmm, yeah. Even once in the barn over a saddle." Dee's whole body trembled at the sensations of a woman's hands and mouth on her as she fantasized about Jake.

Catie grinned and sucked harder on Dee's nipple as her fingers worked Dee's clit. "I'm picturing Jake, his hands clenched on your hips and fucking your pussy until you scream."

The orgasm slammed into Dee, so hard her body bowed, her head thrown back, and a shout tearing from her lips. Catie continued stroking her clit until the last vibrations settled in Dee's body.

"Man that was fun." Catie's fingers slid across Dee's thigh as she repositioned herself in front of the jet spray. "I'm so turned on I'll probably come in an instant."

Still feeling lightheaded from her orgasm, Dee carefully reached out and touched Catie's breast.

"You don't have to do this, just because I did." Catie gave a small moan and squirmed beneath Dee's palm. "I promise I'll still respect you in the morning."

"I want to." Dee laughed softly, enjoying the feel of Catie's nipple pebbling against her hand. "I'm curious, too."

Catie moved her hips against the spray. "In the morning you'll probably blame it on the margaritas and say it never happened."

"I'm not ashamed." Dee lightly cupped Catie's breasts in both hands. "What are you picturing right now?"

"Jess thrusting into me." An almost pained expression came over Catie's face and she spread her thighs wider, taking more of the jet spray. "I'll bet he has a cock worth riding."

Catie moaned as Dee flicked her tongue over her nipple. Hard, yet soft, like a man's erect penis. Tentatively she moved her fingers between Catie's folds that felt like her own, yet different.

With a whimpering cry, Catie came almost at once. Her body jerked and shuddered as Dee worked Catie's clit until her friend couldn't take anymore.

Dee moved away, feeling flushed and tipsy.

"Experimentation is a good thing, don't you think?" Catie asked in a breathless voice when she melted against the side of the whirlpool.

"Can there really be too much of a good thing?" Dee reached for her margarita and downed the last of it as her eyes met her friend's.

"Nah." Catie grinned and grabbed her own margarita. "Not when it comes to sex."

"Even though that was fun." Dee twirled the stem of her glass as her eyes met Catie's. "I still wish I had a man." She sighed. "Like Jake."

"Or Jess." Catie winked. "Having an orgasm is fun anytime. But there's just something about a *man*, you know."

"Uh-huh." With a sigh of contentment, Dee looked up at the star-filled sky. "His hard, muscular body. The way he felt when I dug my nails into his skin. His weight against mine and his masculine smell." She turned to her friend and smiled. "And how good it felt when he was deep inside me."

Catie grinned and flicked water at Dee. "You've got it bad, girlfriend."

Dee splashed water back. "I do not. I'm not going down *that* road again."

Rolling her eyes, Catie replied, "Yeah. Sure."

"Don't even go there." Dee turned her gaze back to the stars. She might enjoy fantasizing about Jake, but that's all it would ever be. Fantasy.

* * * * *

Dee finished applying her mascara and studied her reflection. In just an hour she would be at the rodeo dance in Jake's arms...for *only* one dance. That was it. And then she would go home—and more than likely dig out one of her vibrators.

She usually kept her makeup light and natural so that it hardly looked like she was wearing any. But tonight she'd gone all out—her cheekbones appeared higher, her eyes wider, and her lips more full and sensual. She'd pulled back her hair and swept it up with a pearl comb, auburn ringlets spilling out the top in wild disarray and giving her that sexy just-got-out-of-bed look.

When she'd gone shopping with Catie yesterday, they'd found the perfect outfit. The ivory halter dress was gorgeous and made Dee feel slightly dangerous and very naughty. Sheer netting rose from just above her breasts to the neckline that encircled her throat like a choker, and her shoulders and back were completely bare, all the way down to her ass crack. She enjoyed the feel of the material, silky and luscious against her skin.

Dee smiled as she pulled on the matching bolero jacket, still amazed with what she and Catie had done in the whirlpool last night. And more than a little curious what Jake would think if she invited him to join them in the whirlpool sometime.

The thought gave her pause. Would she want to share Jake with another woman? In any way? *No.*

Wait. What was she thinking? It wasn't like she *cared* about Jake anymore.

She slid her feet into a pair of ivory sandals with three-inch heels and studied her toenails that were painted with pearl polish to match her fingernails. The new garters and thong underwear felt positively delicious beneath the dress. Too bad Jake wasn't actually going to see what she had on underneath.

No, it wasn't too bad at all. She was just going to give him a taste of what he'd been missing all these years. That did *not* include a peek at what she was wearing under her dress.

Well, maybe a little peek.

She grinned and grabbed the purse she'd bought to go with the outfit, then stopped to check her appearance in the floor to ceiling mirrors of her closet door. Tingles skittered through her body and her nipples stood out against the thin fabric.

After tossing her lipstick into her purse, she said goodbye to Blue and strode out the door into the gathering darkness, taking care not to stumble down the stairs in her sandals. The pinching around her toes was a good indication she should've settled for something a little more sensible, but she'd loved the way they looked with the dress.

And at this moment, she felt anything but sensible.

* * * * *

Dee arrived at the fairgrounds and parked the Rover in the dirt lot. When she climbed out, night air chilled her skin as her dress hiked up her thighs. She pulled her skirt back down, locked the SUV, and headed toward the dancehall. Her ankles wobbled as she traveled over the uneven ground and she just hoped she wouldn't sprawl in an ungraceful heap.

Multi-colored lights of the carnival midway illuminated the night. Sounds of laughter and the blare of the country western band filled the air as she approached the dancehall.

Smells of popcorn and corndogs brought back memories of the last time she'd been to the county fair and dance ten years ago with Jake. For the first couple of years after he'd left, she hadn't wanted any reminders of him so she never went to the annual event. And somehow she'd never felt inclined to go again.

Her steps slowed as she got closer and closer to the dancehall, and then she stopped walking and stared at the front entrance, clenching her purse in both hands.

If she allowed herself to get too close to Jake Reynolds, she might start to lose her heart again, and that was completely out of the question. Once was enough for this lifetime.

Okay, so she wasn't as bold as she'd like to think she was.

Chicken-shit.

She whirled to head back to her Rover, and smacked into a solid wall of hard male flesh. Hands grabbed her arms to steady her, and Dee found herself looking up into Jake's eyes.

Too late.

Too late to make her escape, and the most dangerous sensations coursed through her body the moment she found herself in his arms.

Devastatingly handsome, all in black from his western dress shirt to his Wranglers, Jake's eyes were shadowed under the brim of his Stetson and she could see a silvery glint in their gray depths. The musky scent of him surrounded her, making her want him so bad her panties were already damp.

Screw the dance. She'd take him now.

No, no, no!

"Sweetheart," he murmured, the heat of his hands blazing through her jacket. "You look good enough to eat."

"Jake." Dee heard the huskiness in her own voice, and fought to regain her composure.

One dance. That's it, no more. No matter how bad you want to do him.

She put her hands against his muscled chest and pushed away from his grasp, her palms burning from the feel of him.

"Where were you going?" He let his fingers slide down her arms as she stepped back, and she shivered from the sensual feel of his touch through her jacket sleeves. "You didn't change your mind, did you?"

"Of course not." Dee lifted her chin and did her best to give him a flirty smile.

"You want to dance out here under the stars, or go in?" His deep voice was so vibrant, so sexual, that she all but wanted to melt into his arms.

Dammit. You're supposed to be cool, calm and collected and let Jake be the frustrated one.

"Inside." Dee moved away from Jake, and started toward the entrance. She could feel the heat of his gaze on her, and the heat of another kind flaming deep inside.

He remained silent as they entered the dancehall, only nodding to people Dee greeted as they passed by until they found a place to leave her purse. When she slipped off her jacket and revealed the sleeveless, backless dress beneath, she heard a sharp whistle from behind. She couldn't help a smile from escaping.

After she put the jacket with her purse, she turned to see Jake staring at her with absolute lust. He set his Stetson next to her jacket, but never took his gaze from hers.

"Are you ready for that dance?" she asked, hoping her voice sounded steady. Casual. Not like, *I want your hands all over my body now.*

"If it's only one dance, I get to choose the song." He smiled and closed the distance between them. "And I want it to be a nice slow one."

The purr of a cell phone rose up between them, just as Jake reached for Dee's hand.

She took a step back. "Gonna answer your hip?"

"Hold on a sec." Jake gave her a sheepish smile as he yanked the slim phone from his belt. He pushed a button and pressed the phone to his ear. "Reynolds."

Dee watched Jake's eyes narrow as he listened to whoever was on the other end. To be honest she was thankful for the interruption—her body kept threatening to take over her common sense.

"All right," Jake finally said. "Keep me informed."

He punched the phone off and slipped it onto his belt, his eyes focused on Dee. "Now where were we?"

"May I have this dance, Dean?" a man's voice broke in.

She glanced up to see Ryan Forrester, a good-looking sheriff's deputy she'd dated a couple of times. "Why, sure, Ryan."

Ryan gave a nod to Jake, who just scowled and folded his arms as Dee moved with the deputy onto the crowded floor. With effort, she managed to keep her attention on her dance partner as they two-stepped to a fast tune. But every now and then she'd catch a glimpse of Jake's expression, and she had to grin.

A blue-eyed blonde cowboy, Ryan was the big silent type who never had a whole lot to say—which was one of the reasons she hadn't continued dating him. She preferred not to have to carry on an entire conversation by herself. She'd heard he had a little problem with gambling, heading up to the casinos on the reservations whenever he had some time off. One thing Dee didn't find attractive in any man was any kind of addiction, whether it was drugs, gambling, or tobacco.

Even though she had no interest in Ryan other than their casual relationship, she danced with him for two more songs, laughing and flirting with the man the entire time—just to be ornery and drive Jake nuts.

Ryan was smiling and friendly enough, but when Dee asked him if he had any more information on the rustlers, he just shrugged and seemed to become even quieter than normal. If that was possible.

When Dee finally returned from the dance floor with Ryan, Jake's scowl was positively thunderous. It was a wonder the possessive look in his eyes hadn't kept Ryan away to begin with.

She'd barely had a chance to thank Ryan for the dances when Jake took her by the elbow and propelled her from the edge of the dancers.

"This isn't part of the deal," she said when they reached a corner where they were somewhat alone and the music wasn't as loud.

"We have a lot of catching up to do." He leaned one shoulder against the wall, boxing her into the corner.

"What about work? Your calls? You seem to be in demand." Dee tried to sound annoyed.

"I turned it off for now." Jake grinned. "Unavailable."

The wall felt cool to her bare back, and for a second she considered stomping her three-inch heel into his boot to get him to back off. But every sane thought fled her mind as she studied him.

Lord he looks good.

Tremors rippled through her at Jake's nearness, and she wondered how she would begin to walk away from him when that one dance was over. Her body hummed with awareness, as he stood close—not quite touching, yet not far enough away.

"How'd you end up running your dad's cattle ranch?" he asked, that smoky gaze fixed on her.

"I love ranching." Dee shrugged. "I guess you could say it's in the blood." She flattened her palms against the wall behind her. "Your turn. Tell me what you've been up to."

"Had a nice spread in Texas, enjoyed my work and did all right." Jake bent closer, invading her space. No, more like conquering it. "But I was lonely as hell."

She kept her tone light and teasing. "What? No friends?"

"I had friends." He reached up and traced the line of her jaw, his eyes dark and intent. "But something was missing."

At the same moment, the lights dimmed and a slow tune started.

A shiver skittered through her as Jake trailed his finger down her neck. "How 'bout that dance, Dee?"

She nodded. The sooner they got this over with, the better. She'd give him one dance and then get herself away from Jake before she jumped right back in bed with the man.

His hand burned the bare skin at the small of her back as he guided her to the middle of the dance floor where they were surrounded by other couples.

As Jake brought her within the circle of his arms, her nipples tightened. He swept his gaze over her breasts and gave her a sensual smile that caused her mouth to go dry. His hands settled on her waist and moved his hips against hers until she felt his erect cock through her thin dress. Did it ever feel good to have him pressed up against her.

He bent his head next to hers, and Dee automatically moved her hands to his shoulders, letting her body sway with his in time to the music. After the way he'd left her all those years ago, she shouldn't feel so turned on, but lord, was she ever.

"Remember the first time we made love?" he murmured in her ear, and she caught the scent of mint on his breath. She could imagine how good he'd taste and almost moaned at the thought.

"At our hideaway." Dee sighed, shivering at the feel of his mouth so close to her ear.

He pressed her impossibly closer along his solid length, all but making love to her on the dance floor. "It was a clear October day and we went horseback riding in the mountains with a picnic basket, a blanket, and a bottle of wine." His voice was raw, filled with desire. "The sun was shining, and it was still warm enough that you were wearing a pair of tight jeans with a T-shirt. And no bra."

"Good memory," she murmured.

"I could even see your dark nipples through the shirt, it was so skimpy." Jake trailed one finger up Dee's bare spine and she shivered as he continued, "We went to our secluded spot, our own little hideaway, and it was like we were the only two people left in the world. Then you begged me to make love to you."

Dee pulled away and looked up at him. "I *begged* you?"

He brought her back into his arms. "Maybe we both did a little begging."

How Jake's kisses had unraveled her and how badly she had wanted him. *Needed him.* And it was true, she had begged him not to stop.

He had smiled, handling her so gently, as though he cherished every part of her. His mouth had teased her nipples, slowly working his way down between her thighs to her pussy. She couldn't believe he put his mouth on her clit, tasting her until she was writhing, and dying for him to be inside her.

Before he entered her, he had caressed between her thighs until he brought her to orgasm. And then he slid his cock into her, taking her slow and easy. She'd cried out from the incredible pleasure rippling through her body.

He had stopped, afraid he'd hurt her, but she had ordered him to keep fucking her, clenching his hips between her thighs. Harder and faster he moved within her, filling her, until he reached his own climax.

Jake's warm breath on her neck and his low voice brought her out of her memories. "I never thought I could want you more than I did that day. But every day after that, I couldn't get enough of you." His hands moved from her waist, caressing her through the dress, down her hips and back again to her waist. "And somehow I want you now even more than I did then."

God but she wanted to fuck him.

No. She was supposed to give him a lot of hot frustration, not the other way around.

Vibrator waiting at home. Remember the vibrator.

Dee finally found her voice and her willpower. "Nothing's going to happen between us. I agreed to be friends with you. *Not* fuck you."

Jake groaned and pressed her hips harder against his erection. He'd always loved it when Dee talked dirty. Without a doubt, he knew she wanted him with the same fierceness he felt for her. The one dance had already melded into a second, and if he had his way, he'd be dancing with her all night.

And then he'd get her home and in his bed.

Just the thought of what she was wearing under that scrap of a dress was enough to make him utter a primal chest-beating growl, throw her over his shoulder and take her home and do her.

When he'd arrived at the fairgrounds, Dee had pulled in and parked her Rover in the row in front of him. After a moment she'd slid out of her SUV, and her tiny fuck-me skirt had climbed up her thighs to reveal garters holding up sheer stockings. Pure lust had bolted through him at the sight. All thoughts of work, rustlers, and smugglers blew away with the breeze.

Transfixed, as though under a spell, he had watched Dee fix her skirt, raise her head and march off to the dancehall, the best she could in those high heels.

Jake had hurried out of his truck and strode toward Dee, planning to catch up. But then her steps had slowed and she'd come to a complete stop and stared at the building, so lost in her thoughts that he'd been able to get close without her noticing. He had the feeling that if he hadn't been right behind her, she probably would have gone back home.

Now she was in his arms, her scent of wind and orange blossoms flowing over him, and it felt so completely right. He knew he'd been an idiot to leave her, and he damn well wasn't going to make that mistake a second time.

But would she ever trust him again? Well, he sure as hell intended to do whatever it took to earn that trust.

He lifted his head to look down at Dee, admiring her generous curves underneath that skimpy outfit. Through the netting at the top of her dress, Jake could see the mole above her left breast. He yearned to peel away the material and run his tongue over that beauty mark, and every inch of her body.

Dee's green eyes met his, challenging him. "Your one dance is over."

He smiled. "Dance with me all night."

"I—*no*." Her voice was firm as she shook her head.

He brought his lips to her hair, traveling along her temple and down to her ear. "Dance with me."

Dee gasped as Jake nipped at her lobe, and when he raised his head he saw her eyes dark with sensuality and her lips parted. He needed to kiss those lips, to see if she tasted as good as he remembered. His mouth neared hers and she tilted her head to meet him.

"I'm cutting in," a loud voice said beside them.

Dee jumped back and Jake whipped his head up to see Kev Grand. The man had an angry glint in his eyes.

Before Jake could tell Grand exactly where he could go, Dee said, "Why, I'd love to dance with you, Kev."

Jake's gaze snapped to Dee as she pulled away, refusing to meet his eyes and smiling at Grand. Jake could do nothing but step back and watch Dee move into the bastard's arms.

Damn. Fury burned in Jake's gut as he moved off the dance floor toward the refreshment table. He ladled punch into a paper cup and drank it in one gulp, then crumpled the empty cup and threw into the waste bin.

His gaze searched the crowded dance floor, trying to find Dee. He caught a glimpse of fiery hair and a white dress, but she vanished from sight as another couple moved in front of her.

The song ended and lights came up, and the band announced they'd be taking a break. Jake made his way through the crowd, searching for the leggy redhead, but couldn't find her or Grand anywhere. He went back to where she'd left her purse and jacket—but both were gone, along with Dee.

Grand was nowhere to be seen, either.

Knives of anger stabbed Jake's gut as he picked up his Stetson and crammed it on his head. "I can't believe she left with that arrogant, no good son-of-a-bitch."

Chapter Four

🕉

"Thanks for the dance," Dee said to Kev as soon as the song ended, and then she bolted out of his arms.

"Dean, wait," Kev called.

But she pretended not to hear and concentrated on flowing with the crowd leaving the dance floor, and avoiding Jake. If she didn't, she might end up home in bed with him. After the way he dumped her, there was no way she was going to oblige him — no matter how badly she wanted to.

Vibrator, vibrator, vibrator!

The crush of people, along with the sour smell of beer and cigarettes, was enough to make Dee claustrophobic. Her pulse quickened as she glimpsed Jake walking toward the dance floor, his gaze searching the crowd. She skirted the throng, hurrying to where she'd left her jacket and purse, hoping Jake wouldn't spot her. She didn't even stop to put on the jacket, just grabbed her belongings and practically flew toward the doorway.

The memory of Jake's hard body was still imprinted along her breasts, her stomach, her thighs. If it hadn't have been for Kev, Jake would've kissed her and she would've been all over the man and willing to go anywhere and do anything with him. Probably would have fucked him in the back of his truck, outside the fairgrounds.

While she strode to the parking lot, Dee thrust one arm through the sleeve of her jacket and then the other. Darkness closed in on her, the lights from the midway and the occasional floodlight barely enough to see where she was going. Her high heels wobbled as she walked across the rocky lot, and then she stepped into a good-sized pothole.

Dee stumbled and barely managed to keep from landing on her backside. But the twist of her ankle and the immediate, shooting pain of her injury was unmistakable.

Great. Her eyes watered from pain as she wrenched off the sandals and then carried them by the straps as she limped toward the Rover. Rocks pricked her feet, and by the time she reached her SUV, her nylons were shredded, and her thong underwear was riding up her butt and driving her crazy. The comb was slipping from her hair, too, and she yanked it out so that the whole mess tumbled to her shoulders.

"Just peachy." Dee shoved her hand into her purse and dug out her keys. Just as she unlocked the door of her Rover, a male voice spoke behind her.

"Dean."

Dee yelped and whirled around to face Kev Grand, almost passing out from the shooting pain in her ankle.

Holding her hand to her pounding heart, and leaning against the truck, she said, "Dammit, Kev. Don't sneak up on me like that."

"Sorry, hon." Kev' looked her up and down, from her wild hair to her stocking feet. "You okay?"

"I'm not your hon, and I'm fine." Dee shoved her hair out of her face and glared up at him.

Kev stepped closer and put his hands on her shoulders. "We need to talk about us."

Dee blinked. "What us?"

His tone softened and his mustache twitched as he smiled. "You know I care about you. I always have."

"Sure, we've dated a few times." Dee shook her head. "But there's never been anything serious between us."

"I've always been serious about you." He moved so close she could smell the musky scent of his strong aftershave. "I think it's time we did something about it."

"Let go, Kev." Dee pushed her wayward hair out of her face. "This isn't a good time."

Kev moved his mouth toward hers as though he intended to kiss her. Just as she was about to wallop him a good one, a male voice cut into the night.

"The lady said to let her go."

Kev's head snapped up. Dee's cheeks grew hot as she turned to see Jake, his hands in the front pockets of his jeans, and his stance loose-limbed and relaxed. But she knew him well enough to realize he was anything but relaxed—inside he was coiled as tight as a spring, just waiting for Kev to make a move.

Kev lessened his hold on Dee. "Mind your own business, Reynolds."

Jake took a step forward so that he was only a couple of feet from Kev. "Dee *is* my business."

Dee moved between the two men, her hands on her hips. She'd had it with their testosterone laden he-man routines, and the way her ankle was feeling right now, she just needed to get home. "I'm none of your business—neither of you." She glared from one man to the other. "I'll thank you both to leave me alone and to stop acting like a couple of jerks. Get on out of here and go home."

With as much dignity as she could muster, Dee whirled, her sprain screaming with pain. It was all she could do to yank open the Rover door and climb in without them seeing how badly she'd injured her ankle.

She threw her belongings onto the passenger seat and settled herself behind the steering wheel. Her hand on the door, she turned to glare one last time at the two men, and saw them both staring at her.

No, not at her.

At her legs.

Dee glanced down to see her skirt hiked up to her hip, her garters exposed, almost all the way up to her waist.

Heat flushed through her as she slammed the door shut and stuffed the keys into the ignition. The engine roared to life and she threw the Rover into reverse, but stepped on the gas a little too hard. Tires spun in the graveled lot as her vehicle shot back.

And struck something with a sickening crunch.

For a second Dee just sat there, unable to move. Then she put the Rover into park and leaned back and groaned. She had just smashed into someone's car in front of Jake and Kev.

Great.

When she finally looked out her window, Dee saw Jake by her door, and from the quirk of his mouth, she had the suspicion he was doing his best not to laugh. Trying to maintain her composure, she buzzed down the window.

"How bad is it?" she asked Jake with a sigh.

He pushed up the brim of his Stetson and glanced at the rear of the Rover and then back to her. "It's, ah, pretty bad."

"Both vehicles?"

"Yeah."

With a small groan, she leaned over and started digging through the glove compartment for a pen and paper, but could find neither. Her ankle throbbed, she was tired and all she wanted to do was get home.

Dee turned to Jake. "I don't suppose you have a pen and something to write on so I can leave a note for the owner?"

A hint of a smile tugged at the corner of his mouth. He ran his hand over the scar on his cheek. "I've got your phone number and I know where you live."

She frowned. "What difference does that make? I need to leave a note."

Laughter glinted in Jake's eyes and she curled her hand into a fist. "It's my truck you hit," he said.

Rolling her eyes to the ceiling of her Rover, Dee sagged back against her seat. *Perfect. Just perfect.*

Jake studied Dee, watching her hand go to her throat as she absorbed what he'd told her. With her auburn hair in a wild riot around her face, she looked like an angel.

A rather wicked, naughty angel that he wanted to scoop up in his arms and fuck.

Repeatedly.

The sound of a throat clearing reminded Jake that Kev Grand was still behind him, but he ignored the man.

"Sweetheart," Jake murmured to Dee. "Why don't you go on home now and we'll worry about this later?"

Another sigh escaped Dee and looked back to Jake. "I'll give you my insurance info tomorrow. But I need your home number."

"I'll call you."

Her mouth quirked into a tired smile. "All right."

The desire to smooth Dee's hair from her face and hold her close overwhelmed Jake, and it was all he could do to keep his hands to himself.

Instead he put his hands on the door of her vehicle. "Are you okay to drive yourself home? We could always leave your Rover here overnight and I can take you."

That familiar spark came back to Dee's eyes. "I'm fine."

Despite himself, Jake grinned. "I'll talk to you tomorrow."

Without another word, she buzzed up the window and put her Rover into gear. Jake stepped out of the way as she eased forward, the metal on her rear bumper and the front of his truck grinding as they separated.

Grand came up and stood beside Jake as they watched Dee's Rover disappear, minus one taillight.

"Helluva woman," Grand said.

"Hope she doesn't get stopped for that missing taillight." Jake shook his head and grinned. "That would really make her night."

"Uh-huh." Shoving his hands in his pockets, Grand turned and strode into the darkness.

Just as Jake was about to head to his truck, he noticed the dim lights of the midway glinting off an object on the ground where Dee's Rover had been parked. He walked over to it, knelt down and picked up one of her dainty sandals. Chuckling, he took the sandal with him to his truck

It looks like Cinderella lost one of her slippers after fleeing the ball.

* * * * *

The next day, Dee eased back in the living room rocking chair, an icepack surrounding her throbbing ankle, and propped her foot on a hassock as she got ready to mend a couple of things. Sewing was definitely *not* her forte, and the last thing on Earth she wanted to be doing.

Being cooped up inside was a slow form of torture as far as she was concerned. She wanted nothing better than to be out in the barn working with that devil-calf, Imp, or riding Shadow, her gelding, or any number of things that didn't involve domestic chores like mending underwear.

A knock sounded, and Dee shouted, "Come on in."

Her foreman pushed opened the front door. "Got a minute, Dean?"

After she motioned Jess in, he closed the door behind him as he said, "Jarrod Savage, the new Sheriff, says he's personally gonna help us track down those rustlers." Jess held his Stetson in one hand while raking the fingers of his other hand through his sweat-dampened hair. "Thought I'd let you know that Kev Grand reported missing a couple dozen head of cattle, too."

Dee leaned forward to adjust the icepack on her ankle. "So, what did the sheriff have to say?"

When she looked up, she caught Jess staring at her chest. She was braless and wearing a thin white T-shirt, and he could probably see her nipples beneath the fabric.

He cleared his throat and met her amused gaze. "Savage and his deputy figure it's a group out of Mexico. Thinks they're rounding up the cattle late at night and taking them back across the border. That or they've found some place to stash them."

"For what? Money? Food?"

Jess shrugged. "We didn't get that far."

Damn. If they don't have a guess at motive, they're not likely to catch these creeps any time soon. Dee eased back in her rocking chair and sighed. "Anything else?"

"Nah, that's it." He started to turn, then added, "No one can get near that pain-in-the-ass calf of yours. John tried and liked to have gotten the shit kicked out of him."

Smiling, Dee shook her head. "Don't worry about Imp. I'll be ready to tackle working with him in a day or two."

Jess raised an eyebrow. "You sure?"

With a wave of her hand toward the door, Dee laughed. "I'm the boss, right? So get on out of here and let me get this done."

"Yes'm." Her foreman smiled and clapped his hat on his head and let himself back out the front door.

What a fine looking cowboy that man was. Yet now that Jake was back, she no longer felt any interest in her foreman whatsoever. Besides, Catie was so hot for Jess that Dee wasn't about to get in her friend's way.

"I *hate* mending," Dee muttered as she turned to the task at hand and pulled a pair of her underwear out of the sewing basket. It was getting close to lunch, and her stomach growled its complaint. "Now where's that darn hole?" She lifted the garment to where she could see it better in the dim light. It was red satin bikini underwear, one of her favorites, which was why she wanted to mend it instead of tossing it. And besides, it was just a little separation at the waistband.

The only problem was she kept wondering what Jake would think about how she looked wearing them. Though he'd probably prefer her *out* of her underwear.

"There it is." She lowered the bikini and stabbed it with the needle, and heard someone clear his throat.

Dee jerked her head up to see Jake Reynolds standing at the front door, watching her, the corner of his mouth turned up.

Heat flooded through her, a combination of embarrassment at being caught mending her underwear— and absolute lust. He looked so good in a dark gray T-shirt and blue jeans, his hands in his hip pockets, and staring at her from under his black Stetson.

She wanted to climb that cowboy and ride him good.

But what the hell was he doing here?

Dee crammed the red bikini into the mending basket beside her chair, and winced as she poked her finger with the needle. "Ever heard of knocking?"

Jake jerked his thumb toward the outside. "Your foreman said to walk in since you're, ah, incapacitated."

"Oh." The way his voice turned her on, it was all she could do to keep her hand from going to her throat. "Well, don't just stand there. Come in."

Blue followed Jake into the house and she frowned at the dog. "You're supposed to chase off intruders. Especially this one."

Jake smiled, but the Border collie had the decency to look guilty. With his head down, the dog came over to her and nuzzled her hand, begging forgiveness.

"That's all right, love." Dee couldn't help smiling at Blue despite the fact he'd slipped up on the job. He curled up next to the chair and put his head between his paws.

After shutting the door, Jake settled on the couch near Dee's rocking chair. He sat on the edge of his seat, his knee almost touching hers. "Did you ever find out what your dog got into that made him so sick? If that meat was poisoned?"

Pursing her lips, Dee shook her head. "No. I'd sure hate to think that anyone out here was trying to poison him or the coyotes, but it's a possibility."

"You need to be careful." His gray eyes looked concerned. "I don't like what's going on in these parts. The rustling, the poisoning. The mountains behind your ranch, are like crime central."

"I appreciate your concern." With a small sigh, Dee rolled her shoulders. "So why are you here, anyway? I could've given you the insurance information over the phone. You didn't need to drive all the way out here."

He leaned forward, his gaze focused on hers. "Let's go have some lunch."

Dee's breath caught in her throat. "I can't."

"I think you should get out of the house for a while." He glanced toward the door and back to her. "Get some fresh air."

She pointed to her ankle. "I'm not exactly mobile."

The corner of his mouth quirked. "No problem."

Before she could ask what he meant, Jake stood and leaned over to scoop her into his arms. She grabbed him around the neck out of sheer reflex, the icepack slipping off her ankle and clunking onto the floor.

"Put me down!"

"I will." He gave her a devilish grin and strode toward the front door. "Just as soon as we get out to my truck."

"Jake—no." Despite herself, she laughed. "This is ridiculous!"

He ignored her protests and carried her down the front steps. The feel of her body pressed to his muscular chest, and her arms around his neck, sent tingles through her. His elemental scent surrounded her, filling her with sensations of warmth and belonging, like it was right to be in his arms.

Don't even start thinking that way.

As he carried her to his truck, she winced at the sight of the crumpled fender and missing headlight. It was all she could do not to groan out loud in embarrassment.

After somehow managing to open the door, and with more gentleness than she could have imagined, he deposited her on the passenger seat of his truck.

"Where are you taking me?" she asked when he got in on the driver's side and started the vehicle.

He backed the truck and headed down the dirt road. "What would you like for lunch?"

"We can't go to a restaurant." She raised her hands in exasperation. "Just look at me. I'm not dressed to go anywhere."

Jake glanced at Dee and raked her from head to toe with his gray gaze. "I'm looking, and I think you're perfect."

"Yeah, right." Dee's breasts pressed against her tight white T-shirt, her nipples large and obvious. She folded her arms across her chest and started grasping at straws. "I don't want to be carried into a restaurant, and I can hardly go in barefoot."

The truck rattled over a cattle guard as he gave her another wicked grin. "Then I know just the place."

She tried to glare at him, but it wasn't easy. The man was too irresistible. "You're taking total advantage of the situation, you know."

"Yep." Jake pictured that little red bikini Dee had been holding up when he walked into the room, and he wondered what color of underwear she was wearing now. "Got you exactly where I want you."

Well, not *exactly* where he wanted her. Yeah, he knew he was taking complete advantage of the fact that Dee MacLeod couldn't escape him.

She tilted her chin. "Do you make it a practice to kidnap women?"

"Only beautiful redheads with green eyes."

"Uh-huh."

"Do you like ham sandwiches?"

"Love 'em."

"Good. I know a place that makes the best around."

She raised an eyebrow. "A place with a drive-thru?"

"Something like that."

"Humph."

"What are we doing?" she asked a few minutes later, when he pulled up to his apartment and parked the truck.

Jake got out and walked around to the passenger side and opened her door. "Thought you'd be more comfortable at my place." Taking care to not bump her ankle, he scooped her out of the truck, reveling in the scent of her, the feel of her in his arms.

She put her arms around his neck and smiled. "No fair, Jake."

"I know." He loved the way she was clinging to him, her arms around his neck, as though she was afraid he would drop her. But he was real happy at that moment that he had a bottom floor apartment so he didn't have to climb a flight of stairs.

After he let them into his place and shut the door, he took Dee to the lone couch. One-handed he swept the newspapers and magazines to the floor, then eased her down.

"Thanks," she said when he brought in a chair from the kitchen to prop her leg on. She grimaced as she settled her ankle on the chair, and then leaned back into the couch cushions.

Raising one eyebrow, she studied the sparse furnishings and murmured, "I see you go for Early American Monk in your décor."

"Welcome to the dungeon." He tossed his hat onto the only easy chair. "It's temporary until I find some property to buy. My stuff's in storage, so I'm sorry it's not too homey."

"It's very, um, clean." She brushed a rolled up sock off the couch and grinned. "Well, cleaner than your old place."

"Give me time." He chuckled as he headed to the kitchen. "I've only had a week to mess it up."

After rummaging through a box of supplies, he found a storage baggie and filled it with ice. He grabbed a few paper towels, then took them and the ice bag to Dee and arranged it all on her ankle.

"Thanks." She flinched from the pain as she shifted on the couch.

Jake propped her leg on a pillow and rubbed his hand over her bare foot. "How'd you managed to twist your ankle?"

"Those stupid sandals I wore to the dance last night."

Thinking about that sandal on his bureau, Jake said, "I liked them." He gestured toward her foot. "Especially those pearly toenails."

"Good. Then you wear the sandals," Dee muttered, looking up at him with that ornery look he loved. "I've even got some pearl polish left."

Jake laughed, and at the same moment his cell rang. His smile turned to a frown at the interruption as he whipped the phone off his belt and answered, "Reynolds."

"Jarrod Savage here," a deep voice said. "Returning your call."

"Sheriff," Jake replied, and Dee's eyebrows rose. "I called to see how your investigation was going on the missing MacLeod cattle."

"I understand you're with Customs." Savage's tone was even as he spoke. "What's your interest in rustling?"

"A number of factors." Jake turned his back on Dee and headed toward the kitchen. "I'd like to get with you and see if we can make some headway on this situation."

After he'd made an appointment to meet with the Sheriff, Jake opened the fridge and pulled out whole wheat bread, ham, tomatoes, lettuce, mayo and mustard. "You ready for that sandwich?" he called out.

"Sure."

As he threw together their lunch, he asked, "How about some iced tea? And maybe a couple of ibuprofen to go with it?"

"Make that a double on the meds."

When Jake was finished, he took the paper plates filled with thick ham sandwiches and potato chips to the living room and set them on the coffee table. After he retrieved the pain reliever, paper cups of tea and paper towels to use for napkins, he sat at the opposite end of the couch.

"So what was that call all about?" Dee asked in between bites of her sandwich. "Did you find out anything?"

Jake shook his head. "I'm going to meet with Savage on Monday."

"Why are you getting involved?" She bit into a potato chip as she studied him. "It doesn't have anything to do with you."

He set his sandwich on his plate and met her gaze head on. "Sweetheart, if somebody's messing with you, then hell, yes, it involves me."

"Hardly." Dee shrugged and toyed with another chip. "You haven't been involved in my life for ten years. There's no reason to get all wrapped up in my business now."

His gut response was to tell her that she'd better get used to it, because he was in her life permanently from here on out. But instinct told him she'd balk and the last thing he wanted was to push her away while he was trying to gain her trust.

Both were silent as they ate the rest of their meal, and it was a comfortable silence. It felt so damn good being there with Dee. He couldn't help but notice how her snug T-shirt clung to her breasts, and how those tiny shorts covered so little of her long legs.

"You were absolutely right," she said, handing Jake her empty plate when she finished eating. "That was the best ham sandwich."

"My one and only specialty." He set the paper plates and cups on the coffee table. "That and take-out." He scooted closer to Dee, lifting her legs off the chair. As gently as he could, Jake maneuvered Dee so that her back was against the pillowed arm of the couch, her ass resting on his lap.

"What are you doing?" she murmured, her voice low and vibrating straight down to his cock.

"Just want to talk...alone." He brushed his lips over her forehead. "Didn't get much of a chance last night since you ran off."

He started to lift his head, but Dee slid her hands up his neck and into his hair, and pulled him to her. "I've had enough talking."

Chapter Five

ဢ

The instant Jake's lips touched Dee's, his hunger grew, so deep and fierce he knew he'd never be satisfied. Reason went right out of his head and settled way down south, straight to his cock.

Clenching his hair in her fists, Dee ran her tongue over his lips. That sweet, sexy tongue that always used to drive him wild was now about to make him insane.

Soft moans came from her throat as she nipped at his bottom lip. He groaned and her tongue darted into his mouth with her own hunger and need.

He had to taste her. Had to feel her. His arms tightened around her as he explored her mouth with his tongue, plunging in and out, letting her know exactly how badly he wanted to fuck her.

With a quick movement, he took the clip out of her hair and let the mass tumble down to her shoulders. He slid his fingers into her wild mane, picturing them both naked, her hair like flame against his skin.

Dee squirmed in his lap as she kissed him, her round little ass rubbing against his cock. He was so damn hard he was afraid he was going to come in his jeans.

She pulled open the snaps of his shirt, then slid her hand inside, trailing her fingers through his chest hair, across his hardened male nipples, and down, down to the waistband of his jeans.

Before she could go any lower, he caught her hand and broke their kiss.

"I need you," she whispered.

Jake smiled and released her hand to run his finger down her jaw line, feeling her tremble at his touch.

Her eyes focused on him, Dee took his hand from her face and moved it to her breast. "Touch me, baby," she murmured in that husky voice he loved, using the name she'd called him when they used to make love all those years ago.

Baby.

The way the word came out of her sensual mouth, and the feel of her nipple against his palm, just about undid him. Jake had noticed she wasn't wearing a bra, but he hadn't realized just how good she'd feel. The softness, the warmth, the fullness of Dee's breast sent a bolt of lust through his body.

With his thumb and forefinger he teased her nipples through the thin fabric, and then moved his mouth to her breasts. She gasped and arched her back as he licked and sucked her through the cloth.

When her T-shirt was wet from his mouth, Jake pushed it up to expose her breasts. "God, but you're gorgeous."

He caressed the swells with his gaze and his hands, circling the mole above her left breast with his finger. Dee had beautiful tits, large and full, her nipples a deep rose and so hard they were like pebbles. And yes, she felt like satin as he touched her, just as he remembered. "You okay?" he murmured.

"Oh, yeah." Dee's eyes were so dark with passion they almost looked like emeralds. "I want more." She slid her hands into Jake's hair again and pulled him down to her breasts.

He grinned, remembering what an uninhibited partner she'd been. Such a willing and apt lover who'd taught him a few things. It was like she'd been born to love him and only him.

Trailing his tongue over her cleavage, Jake tasted her salty flesh as he leisurely made his way above her breast to the beauty mark. He circled it and then continued his exploration of her body.

Dee moaned and squirmed in his lap, her backside rubbing against his cock. As he moved his mouth from one breast to the other, Jake slid his palm down her flat belly, her skin soft to his calloused palm. He stopped to tease her navel, running a finger around it.

"Baby, you're driving me crazy," Dee whispered while he slowly drew his finger along the silky skin above the waistband of her shorts.

He lifted his mouth from the nipple he was devouring and looked at Dee. "You always make me crazy."

Her eyes were heavy lidded, her lips still swollen from his kisses. "I want your cock inside of me."

Jake nearly groaned out loud. "Believe me, that's exactly where I'd like it to be."

It was all he could do not to rip off her clothes and bury himself in her like he'd dreamed of every day since seeing her again—and many times over the past ten years.

Instead, he took possession of her lips, kissing her hard, thrusting his tongue into her mouth as he slid his hand down her jean shorts to the inside of her thighs. "Spread your legs," he murmured

She opened her thighs for him, and he trailed his fingertips over the denim crotch of her shorts. He traced lazy circles over the warmth, imagining that he could almost feel the dampness of her pussy through the heavy material.

Dee shifted her hips against his hand, but he deliberately took his time. He rained kisses over her face as he moved to unbutton her shorts, and then eased the zipper down.

He moved his lips to her ear as he ran a finger up and down the satiny underwear. "You're so damn sexy, I can hardly stand it." He dipped his tongue in her ear and then nipped at her lobe. "Last night I wanted to throw you over my shoulder and bring you here. I wanted to fuck you until neither one of us could walk straight."

"My fantasy." She laughed, soft and husky. "Being thrown over a desperado's shoulder and taken away to be ravished."

"Desperado, huh?" Jake grinned as he kissed her smile. He slipped his fingers beneath her underwear to tease the curls just within his touch.

"*Sí, Señor.*" She moved her hand to the bulge in his pants. "What's your fantasy?"

"You. And those garters." Jake's voice caught at the memory. "One day you're gonna have to wear them for me, along with that dress." He trailed kisses down her neck. "Promise you'll wear that outfit for me one day. Just for me."

"Yes." She moaned and wiggled in his arms. "Don't stop."

"Lift your hips a little," he said, then pushed the shorts down to her thighs.

Jake raised his head to look at Dee's almost naked form in his lap. She was so beautiful he could hardly stand it. Only the scrap of peach panties covered her, and he wished that he could pull them off with his teeth and then taste her pussy. But he wasn't sure he could hold back if he was between her thighs.

He stroked his thumb along the warm center of her panties, pleased that they were soaking wet. Moaning, she moved against his hand, telling him how much she wanted him to touch her. He hooked a finger under the waistband as she lifted her hips, and slid her panties down until they were riding across her thighs, above her shorts.

Trailing his hand along the inside of her leg, he groaned at the sight of the triangle of auburn curls. His fingers glided into the hair and he cupped her pussy with his palm.

"I can't wait anymore." She brought her hand to his chest and slipped it inside his shirt. "I *need* you to fuck me."

Smiling, Jake moved his gaze to Dee's face and he watched her bite her lip as his fingers penetrated the soft folds of her pussy. She was so wet, so ready for him. Her eyes widened as he slid two fingers into her hot core. He thrust them in and out, just like he'd love to be doing right at that moment, driving his hard cock inside her.

"Jake, *please*."

"Come for me, sweetheart," he murmured as his fingers moved to her clit.

She gasped and arched her back as he caressed her, crying out when his mouth captured her nipple again. He flicked his tongue over it and then the other. At the same time, his fingers coaxed her, urging her toward completion.

When Dee tensed in his arms and Jake knew she was going to climax, he lifted his head and watched her face. Her lips were parted, her lids lowered, her gaze fixed on him. With a shudder and a soft cry, she came. He continued stroking her, not letting up until she cried out that she couldn't take anymore.

When the last golden wave of Dee's orgasm subsided, she realized that Jake was watching her and smiling, resting his palm on her belly, but making no move to go any further.

It felt incredibly erotic with his jeans against her naked backside, her underwear around her thighs and her T-shirt up over her breasts. Her lips tingled from his kisses, and every part of her body shivered with awareness.

Jake looked so good, so sexy with his hair ruffled from her fingers, his gray eyes smoldering. Her nipples puckered as his gaze swept over her semi-naked body and back to her face.

Dee caressed his cheek, his stubble rough against her palm. "Aren't you going to show me the bedroom in this snazzy place?"

"Mmmm." Jake kissed her, soft and sweet this time, his mouth gentle and loving, his earthy smell surrounding her.

His lips traveled to her sensitive breasts and she moaned as his warm breath fanned over them. But instead of devouring her again, he pulled her T-shirt down.

She moved her hands to Jake's shirt, struggling to pull the rest of the snaps apart.

He put his palm over her hands, trapping them against his chest. "No, sweetheart."

"What?" She was still dazed from her orgasm and wasn't sure she'd heard right.

"Your ankle. It's real bad and there's no way that I wouldn't end up hurting you. If you remember, we were always a little, ah, gymnastic together."

Dee frowned. She'd actually forgotten about her injury. The intensity of her desire for Jake had all but blotted out the throbbing. As if to remind her, pain stabbed through her ankle, and she grimaced.

She wanted his cock inside her pussy so bad—the touch of his hands and mouth on her, and that incredible orgasm had only whet her desire. For a moment she tried to think of how they could manage it. But with what she wanted to do to his body, and wanted him to do to her, it wasn't physically possible without taking the chance of wrenching her ankle again.

Dammit.

Jake pulled her underwear over her thighs, his touch sending shivers through her. She lifted her hips as he did the same with her shorts, then he brought the zipper up but didn't button them.

When she tried to sit, he only cradled her closer to his chest.

She frowned. "Let me up, already."

Jake's expression became serious. "First, I need to know we're going somewhere with this. That you're not going to keep pushing me away."

Dee's stomach did a strange flip-flop and her hand moved to her neck. "Are you talking about a relationship, like we had before?"

"Yes." He eased his fingers into the hair at her temple and stroked it away from her face. "Only this time I'm not leaving."

Jake's goodbye rang in her head...*for the best...not ready for commitment...*

She swallowed past the ache in her throat. "How do I know that?"

"You'll have to trust me."

That was asking too much. People she loved, including Jake had let her down too many times. She couldn't afford to care about him that way again. If she did and then he decided he couldn't handle a commitment, her heart wouldn't be able to take it.

Dee sighed. "You really have no idea how much you hurt me, do you?"

Jake's lips tightened. "I know I hurt you. But we were both young. We didn't know what we really wanted—"

"I knew what I wanted. *You* were the one who left *me*." Damn but it was hard trying to talk to him when she was practically flat on her back in his lap.

"We were both just kids, Dee." He released his grip on her hair and ran his hand the scar on his cheek. "I wasn't real good with responsibility."

"That's a load of horseshit."

Jake raised an eyebrow.

"Let me up, dammit."

He studied her for a moment and then slid her off his lap so that she was sitting with her back against the couch. Even though he was gentle, pain tore through her ankle as he helped prop it on the chair in front of her. When she was settled, he sat at the edge of the couch, his hands on his knees.

"All right. What do you need to say?" he asked quietly.

"First of all, we were both adults, not kids." Dee brushed her wild hair out of her face. "You couldn't handle commitment so you ran away."

He stopped and rubbed the nape of his neck. "Look, Dee. I'm sorry. It was that and more. My family doesn't have a good track record at relationships, either. My parents got a divorce when I was a kid, and Nick's marriage didn't make it very far."

"You're not your family."

"I know that *now*." He scooted closer. With gentle hands, he cupped her face. "Start over with me. Let me show you what I've learned."

Dee lowered her eyes, afraid that if she kept looking into that intense gray gaze that she wouldn't be able to say no.

She couldn't allow him into her heart again. Couldn't afford to trust anyone that much.

As she remained silent, he released her and sighed. "I'd better get you home now."

After Jake helped her to stand, he put on his Stetson and grabbed his keys off the kitchen counter.

"I can walk," Dee argued as he returned and bent over to pick her up.

"Riiiight." He eased his arms around her just as the phone rang.

"Aren't you going to get that?"

He scooped her up, looking like he was in a hurry. "Nope."

As he was carrying her across the room, the answering machine clicked on. "Jakey?" a woman's voice said. "Don't forget to buy that hemorrhoid cream."

Jake groaned and stared at the ceiling as the machine clicked off.

Dee grinned. "Hemorrhoid cream, huh?"

"It's because she's such a pain in the —"

"Your mom?"

He opened the front door one handed. "Uh-huh."

"You never introduced me to her when we were dating," she said as he shut the door behind them.

"Now you know why." He unlocked his truck door and deposited her on the seat. "God knows I love her, but the woman lives to embarrass me."

When he went around to his side of the truck and got in, Dee said quietly, "I always figured you were embarrassed for her to meet me."

Jake stopped in the motion of starting his truck and stared at her. "How could you think that? Damn, woman. I was proud as hell to have you. Smart, sexy—warm as a summer night—what guy wouldn't kill to bring you home to his mother?"

Heat crept up her neck, her hand following. "I only felt that way when we were together."

"I'm sorry, sweetheart." Jake brought Dee to him and crushed her against his chest. "I never meant to hurt you like I did. And I sure never meant for you to think you were anything short of near-perfect."

She let herself enjoy his embrace, let herself pretend for one moment that they could go back in time and start over.

But history had a way of repeating itself, and Dee wasn't going to let that happen.

Chapter Six

ဢ

Dee frowned as she watered the houseplants on her front porch, taking care not to bump her ankle as she tried to shove thoughts of Jake Reynolds to the back of her mind. And failed. It was Sunday, the afternoon following the *incident* with Jake.

Her body burned at the memory of his hands and mouth on her, and how she'd begged him for more. She could almost feel his tongue flicking her nipples and his fingers coaxing her clit to that spectacular orgasm.

The memory caused her hand to tremble as she tipped the watering can, and water splashed off the spiked leaves of the spider plant and onto her blouse. She lowered the can and brushed the droplets off her breasts with her free hand, and lightly caressed her wet nipples. The material went transparent, showing her black lace bra and skin.

Dee smiled at the thought of what Jake would think if he saw her damp shirt. She limped on down the line of houseplants and showered the philodendron, the last plant at the farthest edge of the porch. Its green heart-shaped leaves reminded her of the gift Jake had given her their first and only Christmas together. The peridot heart pendant she'd tucked away all those years ago.

With a sigh, she set the watering can down on one of the plant-filled tables. She found a spot on the low porch wall that wasn't taken by a houseplant, and eased onto it, taking care not to bump her ankle. Leaning against a pillar, she allowed herself to relax and enjoy the beauty around her for a few moments.

She had surrounded herself by beautiful living things that she could give love to and nurture. Things that couldn't reject her.

Couldn't leave her.

Wind chimes dangling from the porch's exposed beams made a musical tinkling sound as a light wind kicked up. The breeze teased loose strands of Dee's hair and cooled her breasts where water had splashed, causing her nipples to harden like diamonds. Smells of rich soil and of fall just around the corner filled the air.

Dust churned on the dirt road leading to the Flying M Ranch, and she heard the rumble of a vehicle. She narrowed her eyes, wondering who could be coming over now. Blue barked from inside the house.

The moment Dee recognized Jake's truck, her heart started pounding.

Dammit, she wasn't ready to see him so soon. When he'd brought her home yesterday afternoon, they'd barely spoken. He'd gently settled her into the rocker, kissed her brow and left, with no more discussion about the future.

She gripped the edge of the low wall, clinging to it to keep her hand from going to her throat. Her hold tightened after Jake parked and climbed out of his truck. Why did he have to look so darn good? Why did he have to come back to Douglas and stir up her memories as well as her passion?

Jake strode toward the porch, his walk fluid and purposeful. He hadn't noticed her yet, and she took the opportunity to study the movement of his muscles beneath his white T-shirt and his snug Wranglers. Stubble shadowed his set jaw, his eyes hidden by his Stetson.

Lust. Pure lust was what she felt whenever she saw the man.

As though he'd sensed her, he turned his gaze to Dee and frowned. He jogged up the porch steps and reached her before she had a chance to form a coherent thought.

Her fingers ached from clenching the wall so tight. Otherwise she might just launch herself at him and beg him to fuck her. "Why are you here, Jake?" she asked, trying to keep her voice casual.

He glanced at her bandaged ankle, then back to her face. "You shouldn't be on it."

"I'm fine."

"Like hell." He leaned close and placed his hands on either side of her hips, trapping her. He smelled of sun-warmed flesh and mint, a heady combination that sent her senses reeling. "Do I have to tie you to your bed to keep you off that damn ankle?"

Now there was a thought that made her blood boil. Jake tying her to the bedpost. Naked.

Heat flushed through her and she raised her chin. "You didn't answer my question, Jake Reynolds. Why are you here?"

His face was so close she wanted him to kiss her.

"Satan. That devil-calf." Jake's voice was low and his eyes were on her mouth, but then his gaze met hers. "Figured you might need some help taming him."

"His name's Imp." Dee swallowed, ready to pounce on him. "And I can manage."

"Uh-huh." He pushed away and stood, and air rushed back into her lungs. "When are you going to figure out it's all right to ask for help when you need it?"

She flipped her braid over her shoulder. "I don't need your help."

"One thing hasn't changed." The corner of his mouth quirked. "You're still a stubborn woman."

"Says the jackass."

Jake shook his head and laughed, but then his expression went serious. "I'm concerned about what's going on around here." He jerked his thumb to the mountains behind the ranch. "Do you have any idea how much drug traffic goes through that range? How many undocumented aliens are smuggled across all the ranches here?" He raked a hand through his black hair. "And a good chunk of your herd has been rustled."

Dee frowned. "What do you want me to do? Pack my bags and just leave everything?" She waved a hand toward the bunkhouse and corrals. "This is my livelihood. This is the way those cowboys make their living. You can't just expect me to turn my back on it."

His jaw visibly tightened. "You don't seem too concerned about your safety."

"I'm plenty concerned." A sigh left her in a rush. "And not just for myself — for all the other ranchers and folks who live in these parts. But all I can do is take it a day at a time and hope the law handles the problem."

He nodded, but he didn't look happy. "All right, sweetheart. Want me to carry you to bed to rest that ankle, or to the barn to keep me company?"

Bed. But not to rest — to fuck the hell out of me.

Jeez, all she could think about was sex around the man.

Dee sighed, trying to ignore the tingling of her pussy. "Barn." She knew perfectly well that he'd never leave until he'd accomplished what he came for. "But I can walk."

He bent and rested his hands on her shoulders, keeping her from standing. Heat from his palms burned through her thin blouse and her nipples hardened. Jake gave her that slow, sexy grin that sent every sane thought out of her mind.

His gaze swept over her water-splattered blouse, and he moved his hand across one swell and then met her eyes. "Mmmm, black lace. Do your panties match?"

Those matching black panties were positively soaked. "Wouldn't you like to know?"

"Uh-huh." Jake grinned and placed his large hands at her waist. "Shall I carry you over the shoulder, like your desperado?"

Warmth crept from her neck to her face. Partly from embarrassment that she'd told him her fantasy and that he'd remembered. And partly because she was so incredibly turned on that she wanted to jump him.

A possessive feeling gripped Jake as he slid his arms around Dee. He hooked his arms beneath her knees and she gasped when he swooped her into his arms. Hell, maybe she didn't need to be carried, but right now he'd take any excuse to hold her.

He brushed his nose over her hair as he cradled her. God, but she smelled good. Felt so soft. Her prominent nipples, along with the show of black lace bra through her damp shirt, were almost more than he could take.

Damn if his cock wasn't as hard as a post.

While he carried her down the porch steps and toward the barn, she clung to him. "Jake, you've got to stop this he-man stuff. It's a new century and I'm not some helpless little woman."

Smiling, he shifted her weight as they neared the barn. "How about when your ankle's better, I let you carry me?"

"Now there's an image." She giggled, the sound seeping into his blood like parched desert soaking up rain.

"Watch your step," she said when they entered the barn. "One of the ranch hands did everything but rake the manure in the aisle and muck out the stalls."

The black gelding stuck his head over his gate and whinnied as Jake carefully deposited Dee on a hay bale. Her hands slid away from his neck and along his arms, the light brush of her fingers making him hotter than Arizona in July.

She looked away from him, toward the stall where the calf glared through the slats. "The brat only lets me get close."

"Can't say that I blame him," Jake murmured.

Dee acted like she hadn't heard. "Imp goes berserk if Jess or one of the ranch hands gets near him."

"What do you call what I walked in on the other day?"

She raised an eyebrow, a slight smile on her lips. "Gonna try to handcuff him again?"

"Only as a last resort." Jake went to the rusted and scarred fifty-gallon drum where they'd kept the sweet oats back when he'd dated Dee. When he lifted the lid, the scent of molasses and oats rose up to mingle with the dust, straw and manure smells of the barn. Using the tin can inside, he scooped out some of the feed, closed the barrel and returned to Imp's stall. The calf was the same color of black as the stones called Apache tears, his coat smooth and sleek.

"He's a beaut." Avoiding fresh horse droppings scattered in front of the stall, Jake crouched and set the can of oats down. He eyed the calf, then glanced back at Dee. "How long have you had him?"

"Little over a week ago I bought him from a rancher up north. He's champion stock." She shook her head and smiled. "Right now he's a champion pain-in-the-ass."

"If this guy gets much bigger before you gentle him, he's gonna do more than knock you on your butt."

Dee leaned back, bracing her hands on the hay bale at either side of her hips. The movement caused her breasts to rise and her blouse to gape, exposing more black lace.

A vivid fantasy came to Jake. Of him sitting on the bale with Dee on his lap, wearing nothing but that black lace bra and a pair of garters. Her head tilted, eyes closed, auburn hair falling over her shoulders. Of him thrusting into her core and her riding him hard and fast.

"I just need to spend more time with him," Dee was saying, her husky voice breaking into the erotic video running through Jake's mind.

"Ah, yeah." He barely reined in a groan as he turned his attention back to the calf. Jake shifted so that one knee was on the dirt floor, trying to relieve some of the pressure around his zipper. He had to get his mind off Dee's sexy body and onto helping her tame Imp.

The thought of the calf hurting Dee was enough to sober his lust. He'd known she wouldn't readily agree to his help, but he was sure she'd try to work with Imp on her own. With her sprained ankle, she wouldn't be able to move fast enough to avoid getting seriously injured.

Stubborn woman.

He spoke to Imp in a low, soothing tone, trying to get the calf used to him and the sound of his voice. Imp butted the stall door, his eyes blazing. He snorted, splattering snot on the back of Jake's hand, and Dee snickered.

Jake wiped the snot on his jeans while he continued to talk nonsense. When the little devil had calmed a bit, Jake stood and located the calf's halter. After he tied the end to the stall, he lowered the halter onto Imp's head.

The calf's eyes bulged. He fought and tugged, throwing his weight from side to side. It was a good ten minutes before he finally settled down. His sides rose and fell like a pair of bellows stoking a fire, a wild glint still in his eyes.

"You and I are gonna be more than good friends," Jake said to the calf and then glanced over his shoulder at Dee. "No matter what you might think."

She frowned at the calf, her hand moving to her throat. "You're asking the impossible."

"Nah." He turned and unlatched the gate, then eased it open. "If there's one thing I've learned since I met you, sweetheart, it's that nothing's impossible."

"You always did have a large dose of overconfidence," Dee muttered.

Smiling, he picked up the can of feed and entered the stall, moving slow and easy. He reached into the can for a handful of oats and held his palm under the calf's nose. Imp's eyes glittered and he lowered his head. As Jake started to step back, his boot slipped on a pile of manure. At the same time, Imp rammed his thigh.

The oat can flew out of Jake's hand as he lost his balance. He fell back, landing hard on his ass. Oats scattered, the tin can rattling across the ground, and he heard laughter behind him.

"So much for friends," Dee said.

Jake glanced over his shoulder and saw that she wasn't even trying to keep a straight face. He grinned. "I'm not done by a long shot."

"Spoken like a man who doesn't know when to quit."

"Got that right." He went to brace his hand on the ground, only to have his palm land in something cold and squishy with an unpleasant smell. "Ah, shit."

"Um, are you all right?" Dee asked between more giggles.

He looked up and gave her a wry smile. "Nothing a shower won't cure."

She jerked her thumb south. "Just past Dancer's stall there's a sink and a bar of soap."

After Jake washed his hands, he spent another hour with the devil calf, determined to make some headway in their relationship. Every so often he'd glance at Dee and catch her watching him with expressions ranging from amusement to concern to frustration. And perhaps longing?

Ah, hell. He hurt her bad all those years ago, but he had no intention of hurting her again. Somehow he'd make her see that, and get her to trust him.

For now he was concerned she'd try to tame the calf on her own and end up with more than an injured ankle.

When he finished working with Imp, Jake mucked out the stalls and raked manure out of the aisle, despite Dee's protests. She'd started to get up to help him, and he'd threatened to turn her over his knee.

That shut her up.

This time when he went to Dee to carry her to the house, she rolled her eyes. "All right, Tarzan. If it makes you happy."

He scooped her up, watching out for her ankle. "I thought it was desperado."

She groaned, her cheeks turning a pretty shade of pink. "You're not going to forget that, are you?"

"Nope."

"Damn."

Jake strode from the barn to the house, holding Dee tight. He climbed the steps to the front door and shifted her in his arms to grab the knob. "I want you to promise me something."

A wary look came into her green eyes. "Depends."

He twisted the knob and stepped back to let Blue out. The dog barked and danced around their feet for a few moments before bounding off.

"Don't mess with Imp until your ankle's better. Give it a good two weeks," he said as he carried her across the enormous living room to the rocker she'd been sitting in yesterday.

"You're kidding, right?"

After he eased her down, he sat on the couch near her.

"Dead serious." He leaned forward, holding her stubborn gaze with his. "That calf is a strong bugger, and he's liable to hurt you."

"But—"

"No buts. If I have to play desperado and tie you to your bed, I will."

Dee blushed and Jake had to grin. By the expression on her face, she was visualizing more than what he'd meant by that remark.

Hell, they'd have to give it a try some day. The thought gave him an instant erection and he shook his head. Whenever he was around Dee, he was like a teenager with a permanent hard-on.

She raised her chin. "I can't ignore Imp for two weeks."

He scrubbed his hand over his stubbled cheeks. "I'll come over every day after I get off work."

Dee blinked. "I—that's not necessary."

"I usually get off around three." Jake got to his feet and stood beside the rocker. "I may not make it until later, depending on how things go. But I'll be here."

Another look of protest flashed across her face. Before she could say another word, Jake put his hand over her mouth. Her lips felt soft against his fingers, and he couldn't help a low groan from rising in his throat.

Her eyes widened as he removed his hand and leaned close. He knew he could kiss her and she'd return it. But now wasn't the time, and he wanted more from her than her desire.

He wanted her heart.

"See you tomorrow," he murmured as he brushed his lips over her forehead.

A faint shudder went through Dee, and when he raised his head he saw that her eyes were closed. She opened them as he stroked one finger along her jaw, and he read the desire in her gaze. Before he could step away from her, she had her hands at his belt and was unfastening it.

"Ah, Dee?"

"Just let me see your cock." Her face was intent, and damn near close enough to kiss his crotch as she unbuttoned his jeans and yanked down the zipper.

Jake could hardly think straight with Dee's hands on him, and he groaned. "Don't start something you don't intend to finish."

She gave a satisfied sound as his cock sprang from his underwear. "I'd forgotten how big you are."

"Uh, thanks." His body vibrated with lust as Dee wrapped her long fingers around his thick length.

"I want to taste you," she murmured, her gaze fixed on his cock, and then she licked the head with one long stroke of her tongue.

Every other thought left Jake's mind as Dee swirled her tongue over him, her hands alternating between exploring the soft cloud of hair around his balls and stroking him.

"Come in my mouth," she said, her lips hovering just above his cock.

He groaned grabbed her braid and tugged her closer. She gave a satisfied laugh before slipping her lips over his cock and going down on him. Jake thrust his hips back and forth, plunging in and out of the moist heat of her mouth.

Dee looked up at him while he watched himself slide in and out of her. "I'm gonna come, sweetheart." He clenched her braid tighter.

She answered by sucking him harder, taking him deeper in her throat. Jake groaned as he came, moving his cock in and out of her mouth until she had drawn every drop of semen from him. He was breathing hard and still semi-rigid when he pulled his wet cock out of her mouth.

Dee licked her lips and smiled up at him. "You taste better than I remembered, too."

Jake grinned. "Well, why don't—"

"Yo, Dean?" A man's voice said from behind Jake, coming from the kitchen.

Dee's heart pounded and heat flushed her cheeks as Jake stuffed his cock back in his jeans and zipped them up. He was buttoning them when boot steps came closer.

"Are you in here—" The man's voice cut off and the only sound was the clank of Jake's belt as he fastened it.

"Um, right here, Jess," Dee said as Jake moved from between her and her foreman.

She tried to get out of the rocker, but Jake pushed her back down. "Rest that ankle," he demanded, not looking the least bit embarrassed at being caught at her giving him head.

Well, practically caught at it.

Jess raised an eyebrow, an amused look on his handsome face. "Sorry, boss. Didn't mean to interrupt anything. I'll just leave you two..."

"Jess this is an old, uh friend, Jake Reynolds." Dee struggled to look composed as she introduced the two. "Jake, this is Jess Lawless, my foreman."

"We met yesterday." Jake gave a quick nod to Jess as he rested his hand on the back of Dee's rocker.

With a knowing grin, Jess hooked his thumbs through his belt loops. "Customs, right?"

"Yeah." Dee pushed her braid back over her shoulder. "So. What's up?"

Jess walked closer to Dee and Jake, his grin fading into a frown. "Fence cut along the north pasture and another dozen Angus missing. Our herd's down to two-thirds size."

Dee put her fingertips to her forehead, as if it would force away Jess's words. "We can't afford this. And we certainly can't afford to post twenty-four hour guards around the entire perimeter of a couple thousand acres."

"Found these where the fence was down." Jess reached into a back pocket and pulled out a pair of wire-cutters with a red rubber grip.

"Let me have a look." Jake held out his palm and took the tool from Jess. "Pretty common make and obviously used regularly. The rust says he doesn't take real good care of his equipment—leaves his tools out in the weather rather than putting them away." Jake turned the cutters and examined the blade. "By the wear on this, I'd guess he's right-handed."

"Or she," Dee interrupted. When Jake turned his gaze to her, she smiled. "Hey, I believe in equal-opportunity rustlers, too."

"Could be." Jake's mouth quirked as he handed the cutters back to Jess. "Seems I remember seeing Kev Grand using a pair like this to fix his fence a few days ago."

Dee frowned. "Kev wouldn't be involved with the cattle disappearing. He's pushy and outspoken, but he's just not the kind of guy that would pull a stunt like that. Besides, the damn rustlers are swiping his cattle, too."

Jake had to admit that he'd always known Grand to be an honest man, even if he was a sonofabitch. "Anyone else having problems with these rustlers?" Jake asked.

Jess shook his head as he stuck the tool in his back pocket. "Only Grand, according to Ryan Forrester."

"Sheriff's deputy, right?" Jake folded his arms across his chest. "Met up with him at Grand's."

"Yeah." Jess hooked his thumbs through his belt loops. "The rustlers seem to just go for Black Angus. Kev Grand's the only other rancher who's lost a few head, but nothing like Dean here." A thoughtful look crossed Jess's strong features. "Some neighboring ranches have Angus, but most have Hereford and Brahma. So far none have reported any stock gone missing."

Leaning back in her rocker, Dee propped her throbbing ankle on the hassock. "Sheriff's department is so busy that they're not giving us much attention."

"I'd better head on out." Jess tipped his hat to Dee. "Got stock tanks to check."

A knock sounded at the door and Jess opened it. "Howdy, Catie," he said as he touched his hat, letting the blonde walk through.

"Hi, Jess." Catie watched him leave and then sighed before turning to Dee. Her big chocolate eyes widened. "Oops. Sorry. Didn't know you were busy."

"Not at all." Dee tried not to grit her teeth. She was usually glad to see her best friend, but right now she wanted to be alone with Jake. The taste of him was still in her mouth, and it wasn't near enough.

After Dee introduced Jake and Catie to one another, Jake leaned over and brushed his lips across Dee's. "I'll see you tomorrow."

Disappointment eased through Dee. But dammit, she wasn't going to beg. "All right."

He brushed his finger over her nose and then whispered in her ear. "And don't forget. If you're a bad girl, I'll have to play desperado and tie you to your bed."

"Promise?" Dee asked when he pulled away.

He winked and headed on out the door.

Chapter Seven

๛

Dee paused from mucking out Imp's stall to wipe sweat from her forehead with the back of her hand. A cool October breeze stirred the loose hair at her cheeks and chilled her skin.

It was Thursday, almost exactly two weeks since her injury. Her ankle still felt a little stiff and sore, but as far as she was concerned, she had recovered and didn't need help from anyone—no matter what Jake Reynolds might think.

The rustlers had left her cattle alone the past couple of weeks, thank God. But unfortunately, she'd heard of neighboring ranchers having lost several head of their cattle. When she'd asked Jake if he'd heard any news, he'd just given her his usual answer, "The Sheriff's office is working on it."

Butterflies tickled her belly as she realized Jake would be arriving soon and at the same time, a twinge of regret that they'd come to the end of their agreement.

No. Not regret. She was thrilled that she didn't have to put up with his desperado routine any longer. Dee grimaced and swatted a fly away from her face. *Yeah, right.* In truth, she'd miss having him around.

Imp butted her thigh and she reached down to scratch the calf behind his ears. "You'll miss him too, won't you?" she murmured. The devilish spark was still in his eyes, but he was no longer bent on plowing down anyone who came near him.

Dee sighed and got back to work cleaning the calf's stall. Barn smells of hay, horse and manure comforted her. Much more so than Jake's masculine scent. When she was near him she felt at ease, yet she also felt wild and restless, and more than a little reckless.

Every day Jake had shown up, any time from late afternoon to evening, depending on how his day had gone. Dee had expected — had *wanted* — him to take advantage of the time they'd spent together to try and get her clothes off.

But to her surprise, and dismay he hadn't. He wouldn't even go in the house for a glass of iced tea when she'd offered. He'd spent time with Imp, made sure the stalls and aisles were mucked out, and asked her if there was anything else she needed help with. Then he would brush his lips across hers and go.

Leaving her feeling so frustrated and hot for him, she didn't know what to do with herself. Even though Jake hadn't done more than give her chaste kisses, every minute in his presence was a form of sexual torture.

But damn if she was going to again beg the man to fuck her.

When she'd watched him work with Imp, gradually taming the calf, Dee couldn't help imagining Jake's hands on her instead. His gentle touch on her skin. His lips blazing hot trails over her breasts, his tongue seeking out her nipples.

"Get a grip, Dee MacLeod," she muttered as she raked the manure from Imp's stall and into the aisle.

Dee. It had only taken a couple of days around Jake to start thinking of herself as Dee again.

She realized she would miss more than his masculine presence; she would miss his daily companionship. While he'd spent time with Imp, they'd talked about everything and nothing at all. Jake would share his day at work and talk about his mother and brother. She would confide in him her concerns about the rustlers, plans for upgrading the herd and breeding championship stock.

Talking with him was easy and natural. It made her realize how immature their relationship had been ten years ago. They'd talked, yes, but their relationship had been fiery and passionate, based more on sex than substance.

These last two weeks, about the only thing they *hadn't* talked about was the future of their relationship.

Friendship, she reminded herself.

"Bad girl," Jake's deep voice rumbled behind her.

Dee yelped and spun around, almost clobbering him with the rake. "Don't scare me like that!" She punched him in his muscled bicep and he grinned.

"The deal was two weeks, sweetheart." He took the rake from her and set it aside, then placed his hands on her shoulders. "I've got one more day."

His stormy gaze captured her, and she felt as though she was hovering on the edge of a precipice. Just one step and she'd throw herself over.

She swayed towards him, intoxicated by his earthy scent and potent sexuality. "My ankle's fine," she murmured, amazed she'd found her voice.

He rubbed her arms through the light material of her T-shirt, setting her skin on fire, and smiled. "Humor me."

Oh, she'd like to humor him all right. In the barn, in broad daylight — anywhere.

Jake brushed his lips over her hair and released her to grab the rake. Muscles in his arms and back bunched as he worked, and she barely contained a sigh.

She frowned and moved away. While Jake worked with Imp, she busied herself brushing down Shadow. The gelding whickered his pleasure and lipped her braid. She couldn't help glancing at Jake, watching how gentle he was with the calf.

For the first time in the two weeks they'd spent together, they said little. It was a companionable silence, but she already missed him.

When they were finished, Dee walked Jake to his truck. A breathtaking sunset rode the horizon, gold, pink and purple streaking the sky above the Mule Mountains.

They stopped at the front of his truck. Dee avoided his gaze and trailed her fingers over the repaired fender. "Looks good."

Jake leaned against the hood and into her line of vision. "Did you get the Rover back?"

"Yeah. The body shop did a great job." She shook her head. "I still can't believe I backed into your truck like that."

He chuckled. "If you could have seen your face, sweetheart."

"Glad *you* found it amusing."

"Why don't we celebrate?"

"What?" Dee slid her hands into the back pockets of her jeans and tilted her head. "Backing into your truck?"

"Taming Imp. Your ankle being better." He reached around her to catch one wrist, easing her hand from her pocket and clasping it. His touch electrified her through every nerve ending in her body.

"Dinner, tomorrow," he murmured. "I'll pick you up at eight."

She swallowed. "As friends?"

"Whatever you say." Jake smiled and squeezed her hand. "How's Mexican food sound?"

"All right." Dee pulled her hand away from his, afraid he'd feel her trembling. She made her tone light and teasing. "Don't be late, cowboy. I'll be hungry."

He gave her that sinful grin that turned her inside out. "I'm already starving."

* * * * *

Jake's gut clenched as he drove the last mile between his office and Dee's door. He'd spent the day tracking down leads on the rustlers, but they just kept dead-ending, frustrating the hell out of him.

When Jake had called Jarrod Savage, the sheriff had been out of the office, and Jake had ended up talking with Deputy Ryan Forrester instead. Forrester had been the cowboy Dee had danced with that night at the rodeo dance when she had ended up with a twisted ankle. Just the thought of another man with his arms around Dee was enough to make Jake want to kick the man's ass.

As far as the phone call, Forrester hadn't been much help. The deputy was far too relaxed about the whole rustling situation.

Jake parked in front of Dee's house wondering if any of the local ranchers could be involved. Or was this strictly an outside job?

Whatever the answer, he couldn't give it any more thought. For the moment, his mind needed one thing and one thing only.

After a deep, slow breath, he got out of his truck, headed up the steps and knocked on Dee's door. His throat tightened, and he realized he was nervous. *Nervous*. It was his first real 'date' with her since he'd moved back to Douglas, and he didn't want to blow it.

The past two weeks had been hell, forcing himself to keep his distance from Dee. He intended to take things slow and easy this time. Give their relationship a chance to grow, and give her a chance to trust him again.

But when the door opened and he saw Dee, every shred of his good intentions vanished, replaced by raging desire. He clenched his hands and swallowed real hard.

Dee smiled, her green eyes wide. She'd piled her auburn hair on top of her head in a sexy style that made her look like she'd just gotten out of bed after a day of fucking. The tiny black dress she wore only reached mid-thigh, revealing her long sexy legs.

Legs he wanted to have clamped tight around him as he thrust his cock into her wet core. It was all he could do to keep from grabbing her and taking her now.

As though she could read his thoughts, Dee sighed and ran the tip of her tongue over her bottom lip.

The woman had no mercy.

He reached up and hooked his finger under one of the delicate straps securing her dress. "God, but you're gorgeous, sweetheart."

Dee's smile was seductive. "You sure clean up nice."

Her hand went to that sensitive spot at the base of her throat. His gaze followed, then dropped to the generous amount of exposed cleavage. Her nipples peaked below the thin material, and he had to force himself not to let his hand wander from her shoulder to her breasts.

"Just a sec." Her voice was low and husky as she drew away from his touch. "Let me get my purse."

When she walked to the kitchen, he just about groaned out loud at the sight of her sheer black stockings hugging her shapely legs. A line ran down the back of each stocking—stockings that should be outlawed for what they did to a man. Not to mention those high heels she was wearing. Her outfit screamed sex and he had the erection to prove it.

Trying to gain some control over his body, Jake took a deep breath and thought about work. Thought about anything but what Dee's body did to him.

It didn't do a damn bit of good.

Dee's skin tingled where Jake was touching her elbow as he guided her into *Los Dos Hermanos*, a popular restaurant in Douglas. Sounds of laughter and voices, clinking plates and mariachi music filled the air. Tantalizing smells of Mexican food caused her stomach to growl.

The place was crowded, but they didn't have long to wait before the hostess escorted them to a corner booth. *Serapes* and *sombreros* decorated the walls, strategically arranged baskets of colorful gourds, and *piñatas* swaying from the ceiling's exposed beams.

Jake slid onto the bench next to Dee, his presence solid and virile. When she glanced up, he gave her a devastating smile, and she quivered with awareness from head to toe.

After they had ordered, and the waitress had returned with their drinks, Dee took a long sip of her margarita. The mixture of salt from the rim and the citrusy taste rolled over her tongue. She needed to relax and enjoy the evening, and she was hoping the margarita would help her mellow a bit.

Jake's eyes swirled stormy gray as he watched her, filled with passion—and something else. Something that made Dee wonder if there could be a happily ever after.

Not likely. She wasn't Cinderella.

Though lately Jake had been kind of like a Prince Charming. A devastatingly handsome, untamed cowboy of a prince.

A smile teased the corner of her mouth.

He trailed his finger over her lips. "What's that smile for?"

"It's silly."

"Tell me."

Dee dropped her gaze to her margarita, picked it up and took a healthy swallow. She rarely drank, and she could already feel her body loosening from the alcohol. Maybe it would loosen her inhibitions, too, and she'd get Jake where she wanted him.

In bed, between my thighs.

Heat flushed her cheeks as she looked back to him. "I was just thinking you've been a cowboy Prince Charming these past couple of weeks."

His mouth curved into a slow grin, and fine lines at the corners of his eyes crinkled.

Dee's face grew even warmer. "Told you it was silly."

"Cinderella." His voice was a husky murmur as he stroked her shoulder, drawing lazy circles on her bare arm with his fingers. "Does that mean if I find your glass slipper, you'll be my princess?"

His touch was sensual and hypnotic, stirring her blood, igniting flames throughout her body. She shivered, every fiber of her being acutely aware of him. Wanting him.

Her breasts ached, pressing against the taut silk of her dress. Her naughty stockings and garters felt erotic, and she wanted Jake to explore her body and discover exactly what she wore beneath her dress. She needed his touch, his kiss.

"Watch out." A voice said, breaking Dee's lustful trance. "It's hot."

I'm hot. So hot.

Dee blinked, reality seeping in as she realized the waitress was setting their plates in front of them. Jake smiled and eased his arm from around her shoulder and started eating his combination platter of enchiladas, tacos and refried beans.

So very hot.

Ignoring her own plate, Dee picked up her margarita and took a long draught, peeking at Jake from beneath her lashes.

It wasn't food she was hungry for.

Jake's groin tightened as Dee climbed into the truck cab and scooted next to him. Her orange blossom and rain scent mingled with the smell of his leather upholstery.

As he backed the truck out of the restaurant's parking lot, Dee rested her head on his arm, her body snug against his. The next thing he knew, her hand was on his thigh. Slowly tracing patterns with her fingernail down to his knee, and then higher. Not quite up to his hip, and then back to his knee again.

His heart punched his chest as he guided his truck through Douglas, his body on fire, his cock so hard he could use it as a gearshift. He drove with one hand and captured her wayward fingers with his other. Just as sure as the sun would rise, he knew she wanted him. And he sure as hell wanted her.

She sighed and snuggled closer. "Thanks for the wonderful dinner."

"You hardly ate."

"I'm not hungry for *food*." Her voice was filled with sensual promise.

Jake's erection grew so enormous he was in some serious pain. He wanted to bury his cock inside her more than anything. He wanted to touch her and taste her pussy, and make her scream when she came.

When Dee couldn't dislodge her hand from beneath his, she shifted in her seat, pressing her breasts against his arm. He groaned as she started an erotic assault, nipping at his shoulder through his shirt. She moved her other hand to his chest, sliding her fingers down to his belt.

"Dee," he grumbled in warning and desire combined.

Pausing, she looked up at him. "What?" she asked in an innocent voice.

"If you don't stop that, I'm liable to have an accident."

"Mmmm." She lightly ran her finger over the bulge straining against his zipper, lightly stroking his cock. "Now that would be a shame."

"You're killing me, woman."

Jake wasn't sure how he made it to the ranch without coming in his jeans. Dee hadn't let up and his cock was so hard for her that the minute he reached her house, he wanted to shove that tiny skirt to her waist and take her in the cab.

As soon as he parked his truck and killed the engine and the lights, Dee laced her hands in his hair and pulled him toward her. She kissed him with such hunger that he felt it straight to the soles of his boots.

Lust consumed him as she thrust her tongue into his mouth. God, but she tasted good. Her own unique taste, combined with the citrus of the margarita.

Dee tore her lips from his and rose up on her knees, putting her breasts at the same level as his mouth. "Touch me," she whispered.

Jake's mouth found her nipple and she moaned as he licked and sucked at it through the thin fabric of her dress. He shoved her skirt up to her waist and groaned when he discovered she was wearing garters and a tiny wisp of panties.

"I need to feel you," he murmured as he caressed her hips through the silk underwear. "I've got to taste you."

"Please, baby," Dee moaned as he moved his mouth to her other breast, nipping at it, soaking the thin material. He slid his hand between her damp thighs and she gasped as his fingers stroked her pussy.

While he caressed her, Dee clenched her hands in his hair and rocked her hips. "I want you inside me this time."

"Come for me, sweetheart." Jake sucked her nipple harder and increased the pace of his strokes. "Come for me."

"Jake!" she cried out as her orgasm hit hard and fast.

He continued rubbing her clit, drawing out her climax until she begged him to stop. He slipped his hand out of her panties and she slid into his lap, trailing kisses across his face until she found his lips. Her ass rubbed against his erection as her tongue slid into his mouth.

"Dee," he groaned. He had a wild woman in his arms, and he wanted to drive his cock into her now.

"Fuck me," she demanded.

"God, yes." He yanked up her dress.

She shifted to straddle him—and the truck horn blared so loud Jake liked to have come unglued.

The porch light came on, flooding the truck with light. Dee startled and turned her head to look at the house. Blinking away the brightness, she said, "Who the hell is that?"

He slid her off his lap, adjusted her strap, and made sure her dress was in place. "Looks like a woman."

Before Dee had the chance to say anything else, he climbed out of the truck. Blue rushed up, barking and yelping his greeting. Jake glanced at the house to see the woman's silhouette in the open door.

"Dee, is that you?" the woman called.

"Yeah." Dee raised her voice as she climbed out of the truck cab. "I'll be right in, Catie."

"About damn time," Catie said with a laugh. "I was about to send a posse out to search for you. I'll wait inside," she added and closed the door.

Dee groaned as she looked back up at Jake. "I forgot she was coming over tonight to watch movies."

Jake shut the truck door. "This late?"

"She's always late. I told her to come at nine, and it's probably ten now." Dee shrugged as he slid his arm around her shoulders and coaxed her toward the house. She was unsteady on her feet, probably from the margaritas, and he worried she'd hurt her ankle again. He stopped and scooped her into his arms and headed up the stairs.

"Hey!" She clung to his neck. "No more he-man stuff."

Jake groaned at the feel of her soft body in his arms, one hand on a silk-clad thigh. "Believe me. This *really* hurts me more than it hurts you."

When he deposited her in front of the door, she braced her hands on his arms to steady herself, and frowned. "I'm sorry to end the night like this."

"I wish I could see you tomorrow." He hooked his finger under her chin. "But it's my mom's birthday and Nick and I promised to spend the whole day with her. Then Sunday I've got to take care of a few things on a case I'm working. I'll call you during the week, okay?"

Dee nodded. "Sure."

He smiled and gave her a soft kiss, then pulled away. "The next time we go out, wear that little white outfit you had on at the rodeo dance. I'm dying to see you in it again."

"Okay," she whispered.

* * * * *

Two weeks.

It had been almost two weeks and Jake hadn't called.

And the damn rustlers had made off with another forty head or so from neighboring ranchers, and the damn local law enforcement was ignoring her calls.

And it was just like that SOB Jake to promise to help and then bail when things got rough.

Dee frowned at the ivory halter dress hanging in her closet, tempted to ball it up and bury it in the corner again.

The day after Jake had brought her home from their date, she'd hand washed that darn dress and pressed it. Lust had filled her at the thought of being with Jake again, and she'd needed her vibrator on more than one occasion.

For one brief moment, she'd considered calling him to find out why he hadn't tried to reach her, but pride kicked in. She wasn't about to go begging the man to come climb into her bed and fuck her.

Jeez. What was the matter with her, anyway? She didn't want a relationship and she'd made that clear to him. Maybe he was staying away for that reason.

Maybe he'd found someone else. Not that it made any difference to her.

Then why did the thought of him being with another woman make her feel so angry?

Dee sighed and closed her closet door. She turned and almost tripped over Blue. The Border collie yelped and scampered out of the way, his soulful eyes gazing at her as though he was in trouble.

"Sorry, love," she murmured. "Didn't mean to step on you."

No, Jake was the one she'd like to be stomping on right that minute.

She started to head to the kitchen but stopped at her bureau. As though her will was not her own, she slid open the top drawer, and then the hidden compartment. Inside lay the treasures that meant more to her than anything else: her mother's locket; a black pearl Trace had won at the county fair when she was twelve and had given to Dee; a chunk of turquoise her father had found in Bisbee.

And the necklace Jake had given her after they'd been dating for three months. She had pushed the box way to the back of the drawer all those years ago and had forgotten it. Sort of.

Until now.

Dee wasn't sure why her hands trembled as she withdrew the box. It was rich ivory with the jeweler's name embossed in gold across the lid.

She lifted the cover and caught her breath. She'd forgotten how beautiful it was. The gold chain shimmered in the light, and the pendant almost seemed to glow against ivory velvet. It was a large chunk of peridot in the shape of a heart, bordered in gold.

Jake had given it to her that Christmas. Peridot may not have been considered a precious gem, but the necklace was one of the most precious things she'd ever been given. The gift had come from his heart. He'd said he'd had it made special for her, because it matched her eyes. And since it was her birthstone it would be good luck.

A lot of luck it had been.

She shoved the jeweler's box to the back of the compartment, shut the drawer, and headed out the door. Might as well get some grocery shopping done.

* * * * *

Dee wheeled her almost full grocery cart through the store and stopped to grab a couple of boxes of cold cereal. Her head ached and she wasn't in the mood for shopping, but the fridge and pantry were looking pretty bare.

As she tossed a package of gourmet coffee into her cart, Dee couldn't help again wondering what Jake was doing and why he hadn't called. And why he hadn't taken her up on her obvious desire for him. She'd all but begged the man to fuck her. Twice.

Her cheeks burned as she added a bear-shaped container of honey to her basket and a squeeze bottle of chocolate syrup. Well, it was his loss.

She glanced at her shopping list as she rounded a corner into the sundries department. Just a few more things and she could go home for a quiet afternoon.

Toothpaste and shampoo—

With a crash, her cart collided with another shopper's basket.

Dee stumbled back. Words of apology died on her lips as she looked up to see that she'd just crashed into Jake Reynolds.

He turned from the display in front of him and gave her that slow, sexy grin that made her knees weak. "Got something against whatever I'm driving, sweetheart?"

Warmth flushed through her and she raised her chin. She wasn't about to let him see how much he'd hurt her feelings by not calling like he'd promised.

Her gaze dropped to his practically empty cart and she spied Preparation H amongst the bread, bologna and peanut butter. "Hemorrhoids giving you trouble?" She cocked an eyebrow at him.

He grimaced. "A particularly large one."

The display he was standing next to caught her eye.

Condoms. He was probably stocking up for his current conquest. She gestured to the packages of prophylactics. "Planning on getting lucky?"

At least he had the decency to look embarrassed. But in the next instant his expression turned sensual as he murmured, "You tell me."

"Yeah. *Right.*" Dee clenched the handle of her shopping basket and forced a bright smile. "Well, gotta run." She started to move the cart around his. "See you around."

"Hey." Jake caught her by the arm before she could pass him.

She cut him a glare. "Let go."

Instead of dropping his hand, he rubbed his thumb on the inside of her elbow, his touch teasing the sensitive skin. "What's wrong?" A genuinely puzzled expression crossed his face.

Dee rolled her eyes. "Oooh, let's see. We damn near fuck in your truck cab, you don't call me for two weeks after you said you would, and you expect me to fall into bed with you?"

"I see." His tone was a little hard, his gaze a steely gray. "Lawless didn't give you the message."

With a frown, Dee asked, "What message?"

"I called before I left, but your foreman answered the phone and said you were checking stock tanks." Jake released Dee's arm and leaned against his shopping basket. "At the last minute I was sent to California to help break up a major smuggling ring with ties to a case I've been working on here. I got back late last night."

"Oh. It must have slipped Jess's mind." Heat crept up her neck toward her cheeks. Her anger with Jake died like flames under a downpour.

Did Jess forget?

Did he forget on purpose?

Didn't matter. She'd just kill the man and have done with it, dammit.

Two weeks of suffering, of being angry for nothing. Dee's rage faded to embarrassment.

"I've missed you." The way Jake stared at her cleared everything up, straightaway. She felt calm again, then agitated right away, then…wet with lust. "I'd planned to call you today after I got a few things for my mom."

She nodded, not sure what to say.

"I want to take you someplace special." He moved closer, just inches away. "Tonight."

Her body quivered at his nearness, and she bit her lip. She'd spent the past two weeks telling herself it was for the best he hadn't called. It was dangerous to be around the man too much. She kept losing her head, and he made her long for things she knew better than to wish for.

"Dee?" he murmured.

The sound of his voice, his earthy scent and raw masculinity made her wild. She needed to tell him no. Not now, not ever. "What time?"

"Is seven too early?" The pleasure in his expression was unmistakable.

"That sounds fine." Dee swallowed. "Casual?"

"No. Dress sexy. I want to see what I've been waiting for." His gaze was so filled with desire that her breasts were positively aching and her panties soaked.

God, she had to fuck him.

And soon, before she lost her mind.

Dee gave Jake a seductive smile and leaned past him to grab a box of extra-extra large ribbed condoms and tossed them into her basket.

She touched her fingertips to his jaw and pushed it closed. "Don't be late," she murmured and wheeled her cart to the checkout counter.

Chapter Eight

ဆာ

Frowning, Dee studied her reflection in her bedroom mirror. "Maybe I should wear something else."

"That dress says exactly what you want." Catie grinned as she handed Dee her brush. "Fuck me, baby."

"And I aim to get it tonight." Laughing, Dee ran the brush through her hair, the auburn mass falling wildly around her face and shoulders.

Although for the thousandth time, Dee wondered if she was making a mistake by going out with Jake.

Well, why the hell not? Why couldn't she just enjoy the man and his body while it lasted? Enjoy the ride, knowing that eventually she'd have to get off.

As much as a part of her wished for something more permanent, she refused to give in to those dreams Jake had said about wanting to start over, but she'd decided long ago—and was now frequently reminding herself—that she wouldn't trust her heart and soul to anyone again. Period.

"When's he supposed to be here?" Catie plopped onto the edge of Dee's bed, her hands braced behind her.

Pursing her lips at her reflection, Dee put a touch of peach lipstick. "Anytime now."

"So how would you rate Jake in bed in comparison to other guys you've been with?"

"I can't." Dee gave a little shrug and dabbed orange blossom perfume on each wrist. "I don't have anyone to compare him with."

Catie's voice rose, her tone incredulous. "Are you saying that he's the *only* man you've actually fucked?"

"Well…" Dee grabbed her purse and dropped her lipstick inside, her eyes avoiding Catie's chocolate gaze. "I've only gone so far with other guys, and then I—I freeze up." She shoved her hair out of her face and looked at her friend. "Maybe I *am* an Ice Queen like everyone thinks."

A man's voice rumbled, "I know for a fact you aren't."

With a yelp, Dee whirled toward the door, knocking her purse and all its contents across the floor. Heat flooded her as her eyes locked with Jake's.

He was leaning up against the doorframe, his arms folded across his broad chest, and his gaze focused intently on her. She was ready to die of embarrassment at him overhearing that he was the only man she'd ever had sex with—that was not something she'd *ever* intended to let him know.

Yet his sensual smile and smoldering gray eyes made her stomach flutter in anticipation. He was wearing his black Stetson, an ivory western dress shirt with pearl snaps, snug jeans and boots. And damn if she didn't want to eat him up whole, right then and there.

"Hi." Catie bounced off the bed and extended her hand toward Jake, giving it a quick shake before dropping it. "I'm Catie, and I dare say you could only be Jake."

"Pleasure." His sexy grin and the rumble of his voice made Dee's nipples tighten, and all she could think about was being alone with him. Naked.

Catie grinned at Dee over her shoulder and said, "Hot tub. Definitely," before turning back to Jake. "I was heading on out. You two have fun."

"See ya, Sweetpea," Dee called after her friend as she knelt down and gathered the scattered contents of her purse.

As Dee heard the front door open and shut, Jake crouched beside her and said, "Hot tub?"

"Oh, nothing." Just the thought of having Jake in the whirlpool with her made Dee's mouth water. But she still would not want to share him in any way with another woman. Even just playful sex with her best friend?

The answer came through loud and clear. *No.*

"Ready to go?" he said in a husky murmur, his gaze raking over her as he handed Dee the tube of lipstick and her compact. "Or are you planning to go barefoot?"

"Oh." Heat burned Dee's cheeks as she stuffed everything back into her purse. "I'll grab some heels."

Jake reached back and pulled Dee's sandal out of his hip pocket. "Missing this?"

Her eyes widened as they stood. "How did you get it?"

"You dropped it by your Rover the night of the dance. I found it after you left."

"I can't believe you've had my shoe all of this time." Dee smiled at Jake and grabbed the other sandal off the top of her dresser. "I'll get these on and then I'm ready."

Was she ever ready. She wanted him bad. Right now.

Jake moved so close that she could feel his heat radiating through her. "Let me see if the shoe fits, Cinderella."

She tilted her head, her heartbeat accelerating. "And if it does, will you be my cowboy prince?"

Her insides melted as he gave her that drop-dead gorgeous grin of his. "If you want me to be."

"Yes," she whispered.

Dee reached for the sandal, but he shook his head. "No, the prince gets to try it on you." Before she could respond, he maneuvered her onto the edge of her bed, and knelt down in front of her.

He rested his hands either side of her hips, his mouth so close to hers that she could feel the warmth of his breath on her lips. Blood rushed in her ears and her throat went dry.

His eyes slowly traveled down her dress, and her gaze followed his. From her prominent nipples puckering the front of the dress, to her flat belly, down to the garters exposed below the hem of her skirt that had hiked up to the top of her thighs.

Slowly, he slid one finger from her hip, over the exposed skin above the garter, and onto the sheer stocking. Dee gulped, her breathing coming hard and fast, her panties already soaking.

Continuing on down her thigh in that maddening pace, Jake trailed his finger over her knee, down her shin to her ankle. He caught her heel in his hand, tracing the ball of her foot and then raised it to his mouth.

She gasped as he ran his tongue along her arch. The feel of him through her sheer stockings was incredibly erotic. It made her hotter and wetter, and so ready for him to fuck her.

He nipped at her big toe and then sucked on it, and she thought she was going to climax from the feel of her toe in his warm mouth. She whimpered when he pulled away and slipped the sandal onto her foot.

Jake let her foot slide out of his grasp, then reached up to tug the other sandal out of her hand. The movement startled her. She'd been so intent on what he was doing, she'd forgotten that she was holding it.

Smiling, he ran his fingers down her other leg until he reached her stockinged foot. He caressed it as he had the other, with his tongue and his mouth, and then slid the sandal on. When he was finished, he brought his gaze to her face.

Nudging her knees apart, Jake moved between her thighs, and forced her back so that she was partially reclining and bracing her arms on the bed behind her. He pressed against her until the bulge in his jeans was tight against the wet crotch of her panties. His face was an inch from hers, yet he made no move to kiss her. He ground his cock harder against her pussy, spreading her thighs farther apart.

Dee moaned as he nuzzled her neck, the feel of his stubble against her skin lighting a fire inside her.

Just as she was about to beg him to fuck her, he pulled away. "I made reservations in Bisbee. We'd better leave if we're going to make it on time."

Surprised and disappointed, Dee only nodded. She wanted him bad. And she wanted him now.

* * * * *

Jake held his hand against the small of Dee's bare back as the waiter led them to an obscure corner of the restaurant.

This time, the cell phone was off. He'd even left the damn thing in his car. Let the rustlers take all the cattle in the county. Tonight, his attention belonged to Dee.

Her skin felt hot against his fingertips, and he yearned to peel her clothes off and slide his cock into her.

Right there, on the restaurant floor.

It had been one incredible feat of self-control to not take her the moment he got to her house. But he didn't want her thinking this was only about sex, even though that's all she seemed to want from him.

As they walked across the plush burgundy carpet and through the maze of mauve draped tables, he wondered what it would take to get Dee to trust him again. This morning at the grocery store it had been obvious that she was a long way from that point.

When they reached the table, the waiter stood politely by as Jake and Dee were seated. A single candle flickered at the center of the table, barely giving enough light to see by. The restaurant was busy, but the way their table was hidden from view in the corner, they might as well have been alone. Which was just fine with Jake.

Dee set her purse and jacket down then slid into the cozy booth, trying to keep that scrap of a dress from climbing up her thighs.

Let it climb, sweetheart, Jake thought. *Let it climb.*

Scooting next to her, so that his leg was pressed against hers, Jake whispered in her ear, "It's so dark no one can see, and the table hides you from view."

His gaze roamed over her, and then he added, "From everyone but me, that is."

"If you say so." Dee gave him a wicked smile and stopped trying to pull her skirt down. Instead, she wiggled and let her dress hike up to the top of her thighs.

Jake's cock had an immediate reaction to the sight of those garters, and he was real glad the waiter couldn't see either one of their laps.

The ponytailed waiter handed them each a menu. After they ordered the shrimp appetizer, main course, and their drinks, the waiter left them alone. But a second later, a busboy placed glasses of ice water in front of Dee and Jake.

"Romantic." Dee picked up her glass and sipped her ice water, glancing around the restaurant.

"Uh-huh." Jake's mind was mush and he could hardly take his eyes off her.

Dee's scent of rain and orange blossoms enveloped him, sharpening his senses. Her thick hair fell like molten copper over her shoulders, resting on the top of her breasts. Candlelight reflected in her eyes and her lips were glossy and slightly parted.

The thought of what she could do with those lips darn near made Jake groan aloud. While he'd been gone, all he'd thought about was how much he'd enjoyed their time together when he'd been working with Imp, and how he wanted to see her.

The waiter returned with their drinks and vanished again into the restaurant's darkness. Jake found himself wishing the guy would stay away. At least long enough for him to steal a kiss from Dee. Or two.

To hell with the waiter.

Dee picked up her glass of white zinfandel and smiled. Through the crystal wine glass he saw her tongue press against the rim, the rose fluid rolling over her lips. Mesmerized, he watched her throat as she swallowed.

He swallowed, too. His throat was so dry he didn't think he could have spoken a word.

Forcing himself to move, Jake picked up his draft and downed half the glass before letting himself look at Dee again.

The sensual play continued until the smell of grilled shrimp alerted Jake that the waiter had brought the plate of appetizers they'd ordered. Dee picked up a shrimp and peeled off the tail. Then she held the morsel between her thumb and forefinger and placed it in front of Jake's lips.

"Open up," she murmured and slipped the shrimp into his mouth when he complied. Jake sucked her fingers as she withdrew them and he felt the slight tremor of her hand.

"The taste of you was the best part," he said as he selected a shrimp. Her eyes focused on him, she parted her lips. As he put the shrimp into her mouth, she caressed his fingers with butterfly strokes of her tongue.

Just from what Dee was doing with that incredible tongue, Jake's cock was so hard he thought he might come in his jeans.

She brought another shrimp to his mouth and his gaze strayed to her breasts. He suckled her fingertips like he wanted to be doing to her prominent nipples. Slow lazy strokes and then harder, applying slight suction.

Too soon, or maybe not soon enough, the shrimp were gone. Dee licked her own fingers as she stared at him, the candlelight reflecting desire in her green eyes.

The waiter arrived with their meals, but they barely noticed.

Jake had never had a meal that was a sexual experience like this one. Every bite Dee took made him feel as though she was thinking about going down on his cock, licking her tongue along his length and swallowing his come.

She continued to feed him bites of grilled chicken with her fingers, and he returned the favor, until their plates were clean.

"Dessert?" the waiter asked when he cleared their plates away.

Frankly Jake wanted to get out of the restaurant and out to his truck. He'd never fucked in the cab before, but at the moment it was looking real good.

Dee glanced up from the dessert menu and licked her bottom lip. "Why don't we share a piece of chocolate cheesecake?"

Jake could hardly form a coherent thought as all his blood had pooled in his groin, so he settled for a quick nod.

In a few minutes, the waiter returned with the slice of cheesecake and set it in front of them with two forks. Raspberry sauce drizzled down one side of the dessert.

Dee dipped her finger in the sauce and sucked it off. "Mmmm, this is heaven."

Jake thrust his fork into the cheesecake. "I know what's even better."

She gave him a seductive smile. "Oh, you do?"

Holding the bite of cheesecake in front of her lips, Jake's right hand glided up her thigh, over the silky stockings, and to the bare flesh above.

She gasped as his hand traveled beneath her skirt to the wisp of satin panties beneath. "Jake," she whispered, but he slipped the bit of cheesecake into her mouth.

"Better than cheesecake." He skimmed the crotch of her panties, and smiled when he felt how damp they were. He found the edge of the fabric, and her eyes widened as his fingers brushed over the curls beneath.

Her hand trembled as she put her own fork into the dessert and she held it up to his lips. The cheesecake was smooth and creamy and melted over his tongue as his fingers glided into the wetness of her pussy. He wanted nothing more than to taste her right now instead of that cheesecake.

"If you keep doing that," Dee said with obvious difficulty, "I'm going to come right here in the restaurant."

"That's the idea." Jake fed her another bite of cheesecake as he continued to rub his finger over her clit. "No one can tell what we're doing."

He looked into her eyes, the passion in them driving him wild. "I want to watch you come, sweetheart. Now."

In the next moment her hand was in his lap, caressing his cock through his jeans. He thrust his fork into the cheesecake again, then slid the bite into Dee's warm mouth just as she parted her lips and climaxed.

Her body shuddered with wave after wave of her orgasm. He didn't let up stroking her until the tremors stopped and she relaxed against the back of the booth.

"*Oh. My. God*," she said, her eyes rolling back. "Unbelievable."

Watching Dee come had damn near put Jake over the edge. She continued to stroke his cock as she looked at him with heavy lidded eyes. He slipped his hand out of her panties and placed his palm over hers, stopping the motion that was driving him over the edge.

With a shaky sigh, she sat up in her seat. Her hand trembled as she picked up her glass of wine. "I'll never think of chocolate cheesecake in quite the same way," she murmured over the rim of her glass, and then drained the contents before setting her glass down.

"Me neither." Jake smiled and kissed her, licking away a bit of raspberry sauce from the corner of her mouth.

The waiter approached and set the check on the table. "Anything else I can do for you?"

Dee shook her head and Jake said, "We're more than fine."

"Thanks. Please come again."

Dee burst into a fit of giggles and Jake grinned. "I'm sure we will."

With a puzzled smile, the waiter took their empty dessert plate and left. Jake pulled cash out of his wallet and put it in the center of the table with the bill.

Dee dabbed her lips with her napkin, and then tossed the napkin under the table.

Jake raised an eyebrow. "What did you do that for?"

She winked. "Oops. I dropped my napkin. Better get it."

Before he could say a word, she slid beneath the tablecloth.

Blood pounded in Jake's ears. Dee wasn't about to do what he thought she was.

"Ah, Dee?" he said as she disappeared.

She pushed the tablecloth out of the way and moved between his thighs. "I'm going to return the favor."

Jake's breathing became ragged and his hard-on positively ached. "Here?"

"Mmmm." Dee's nimble fingers found his belt and she undid it in record time. "You said no one could see us. And the waiter left the check, so he's not likely to come back right away. But *you'll* come." Her words were slightly muffled, but the sensual tone was unmistakable.

Jake felt a tug on his zipper, and then thrill and release as his throbbing cock sprang free.

His eyes darted around the restaurant.

No one could see them.

Right?

God, he hoped not.

And then he couldn't think any more as Dee's hot breath teased him. Slowly, she slid him into her mouth, flicking her tongue around the head of his cock.

He groaned then bit the inside of his cheek, fighting to hold back the next groan.

As if sensing her advantage, Dee went down on him, taking in his full measure.

God, her mouth was warm. Hot. Burning.

Jake slipped a hand beneath the tablecloth and clenched her hair in his fist. There was something about sitting in a restaurant and not being able to see what she was doing to him that made the entire experience beyond erotic.

He chewed his cheek to the point of blood, holding back another groan as Dee stroked him with her hand and mouth, sucking and licking him. Her other hand found the soft sack behind and caressed his balls.

Intense sensations flooded Jake. "Dee... My God."

He'd never felt anything like this. Not even close.

Fighting to keep his eyes open, to be sure no one was about to happen upon them and haul them straight off to jail, he gave himself up to Dee's hot mouth.

He couldn't help it. Sweet Jesus. What was she doing to him?

Sweat broke across his forehead as Dee took him deep in her welcoming throat. So soft. So wet.

In the next instant, Jake's body corded. He clenched his teeth to hold back a shout as he came. She grabbed his hips and held him at the back of her throat, swallowing his semen until the last surge of his orgasm ended.

His vision was still a little hazy when he noticed the waiter approaching. Dee started to get up but Jake leaned closer to the table and pressed down on her head with his palm.

"Waiter," he mumbled, and heard her soft laugh from between his knees.

When the waiter reached the table, his gaze flicked to Dee's empty seat and then to the cash.

"Keep the change," Jake managed to say, his jaw twitching as he felt Dee's hand caressing his cock. Up and down. Slowly. Teasing him, wanting a repeat.

And damned if he wasn't getting hard again.

"Thanks," the waiter said as he picked up the money. "Have a good one." With a slight inclination of his head he turned and left.

"Oh, I did," Jake murmured under his breath.

His hands slid back to Dee's hair. He tried to pull her up, but she wasn't budging.

Slowly, her tongue worked him again, from top to bottom.

He was pouring sweat now, and his body jerked as she closed her lips over him once more and coaxed his hardness back into her mouth. Sucking. Just the right pressure. Just the right soft brushing from her teeth.

Her hands traveled to his hips, forcing him forward as her sucking became more demanding. More insistent.

Jake let go of her and grabbed the table.

"Damn," he whispered. "Damn, woman. Have you lost your mind?"

Dee purred, and the rumble of her voice against his now-throbbing shaft was too much to bear.

Jake closed his eyes.

Let the whole restaurant know. He could care less. All that mattered was Dee's mouth. The rhythm of her ceaseless caress, her throaty welcome as she took him in, up and down, harder and faster.

The table rattled as he came, unable to hold back a fresh round of groans. His face burned, and he coughed, trying to cover up the sound.

Mercifully, she kissed him a few more times, then stopped. He felt her tucking his still semi-hard cock back into his shorts, and heard the soft hum of the zipper of his jeans, and then she fastened his belt buckle.

Once more, his hands found Dee's hair and ran down her body as she rose from under the tablecloth to her seat. She grinned and dabbed her lips with the napkin.

"Found it," she said.

Jake opened his mouth, but all that came out was a rattling sigh of exhaustion. He felt like he could fall asleep on the table. Face first. But he didn't dare. Who knew what Dee might do to him then?

She grinned at him, letting the napkin fall across his shaking hand. "Maybe you ought to be more careful starting things you can't finish in public, Jake Reynolds."

"I'll keep that in mind." His voice sounded like gravel in a box.

Dee shook her head and wrapped her arms around his neck. "You're still the most exciting man I've ever met."

He pressed his lips to her forehead. "And you're dangerous, sweetheart."

Her green eyes glittered, and she kissed the corner of his mouth. "I love how you taste." She released her hold around his neck and checked the zipper on his jeans. "You ready to leave, baby?"

Jake wasn't too sure he could walk straight after that, ah, mind-blowing experience, but he cleared his throat and nodded. "Yeah. Let's get you out of here before you drop anything else."

Chapter Nine

🔊

Contentment settled throughout Dee as Jake drove them back to the ranch. She couldn't believe how incredible her orgasm had been, heightened by being in a public place and the danger of getting caught.

Oh, and how she'd enjoyed giving Jake his dues, taking his cock in her mouth under that table. The power she'd had over him had been intoxicating. It had been incredible feeling his release as he came in her throat, and how she loved making him come twice in one sitting.

Did she dare go for a third? She so wanted to ride that cowboy, and ride him good and hard.

A country tune played on the radio as she studied his features in the amber glow of the dashboard lights. So gorgeous. That rugged profile, the cleft in his chin, the strong line of his jaw. His big hand gripping the steering wheel and the bit of hair curling around the cuff. Just looking at him made her pussy ache.

"Penny?" she asked him, a husky catch to her voice.

For a second Jake took his attention from the road and gave her a grin that melted her insides. "You."

Dee smiled and slid her hand down his thigh. "Yeah?"

He nodded, his gaze fixed on the road. "How is it that no other man managed to get you into his bed?"

Damn. Her hand stilled and she cleared her throat. "Oh. You heard that comment, too."

"Uh-huh."

What the heck. With a shrug, Dee said, "I came close a couple of times when I went away to the university, but I just couldn't bring myself to go all the way." She paused and brushed her hair away from her face with a free hand. "And here, well, I've been too busy running the ranch and just hadn't met the right man."

Jake cut her a look that she couldn't read. "You haven't dated anyone around here?"

"Oh, I've dated." Dee stroked his thigh again, from his knee to the crease at his hip, and back to his knee. And if she wasn't mistaken, that bulge in his jeans was getting bigger by the second. "I've just never been inclined to let it go that far. I sorta freeze up."

"There's nothing cold about you, sweetheart." He shifted in his seat. "All that incredible sexual energy, pent up."

Dee smiled and lightly skimmed his groin with her nails. "You complaining?"

Groaning, Jake moved his hips against her fingers. "Ah, no."

Oh, baby. He was definitely getting rock-hard.

"What about you?" She trailed her fingers up his flat muscular belly. "Have you dated a lot?"

Jake shrugged, keeping his eyes focused on the road and looking distinctly uncomfortable. "Some. Never seriously."

Dee moved closer, breathing in his musky scent, and traced his nipple through his shirt. "And sex?"

He groaned again. "Why don't we change the subject?"

She slid her hand back down his stomach to the waistband of his jeans. "Why? You asked me, and I was honest about it." Though Lord knows he would never have known if she hadn't been so stupid as to blurt it out to Catie in the first place.

Dee settled her fingers on his bulge and lightly squeezed his cock. "So, tell me."

His jaw tightened and he moved his hips against her hand. "A couple of times."

Yeah, right. And she was the Queen of the Nile.

Maybe she should have experimented and had sex with different guys so she'd have something to compare. She'd honestly intended to, and wanted to, but no man had ever turned her on the way Jake did. Every time she came close to having sex with a guy, she'd compare the man with Jake and would find herself growing cold. She'd begun to think that she was frigid — as had some of the men she'd dated.

Jake had ruined any possibility of her enjoying sex for the sake of sex — with anyone but him.

She squeezed and caressed Jake through his jeans as she studied his handsome profile. That's what she needed to do to get him out of her system — to take him deep inside her and fuck him good. She'd enjoy the ride and then get off. But this time with her eyes wide open, knowing it wouldn't last — unlike the last time when she thought he'd be with her forever.

Jake turned his truck onto the dirt road that led to the Flying M Ranch. "Penny?" he asked as they neared her house.

I'd like to fuck your brains out.

"Mmmm, nothing."

Dee abandoned her attack on his lap as they pulled up to the ranch house. Jake parked the truck and killed the engine.

The instant his hands were off the steering wheel, he cupped the back of Dee's head and brought her roughly to him. She gasped as his tongue thrust into her mouth, his lips grinding against hers. His free hand slipped inside her halter dress, where he captured her breast and squeezed and fondled it.

When he lifted his head to look at her, his breathing was rough and his expression possessive. "Damn but I want you, woman."

Dee moved her lips to his ear and whispered, "Fuck me, Jake."

The rumble in his chest was deep, untamed. "Let's get in the house." With a jerk he opened the truck door and climbed out in a hurry.

Jake might want to wait to get in the house to fuck, but Dee had other plans.

As she followed him out the driver's side door, she intentionally let her skirt slide up her hips as she climbed out of the cab. She was facing him, her garters exposed almost up to her thong underwear.

Jake braced his hand against the truck door, staring at her thighs as though he'd lost his brains. Well, she knew right where they'd gone. South. The perfect place to screw them out.

"Oops. Forgot my things." She turned and bent over the seat as she reached for her purse and jacket, her skirt hiking up even further. Cool air caressed her backside, which was bare thanks to the thong underwear, and she knew she was giving him a great view. She wiggled her hips and parted her thighs, letting the dress shimmy up a little more.

From behind she heard his groan, and then his warm hands pushed her dress up around her waist, completely exposing her naked bottom.

"Jake," she murmured as he caressed her bare flesh, his hands rough and possessive. "What are you doing?" As if he wasn't doing exactly what she had wanted him to do.

"You drive me out of my mind, woman," he murmured as he settled against her, his jeans rough against her flesh.

Oh, how hard his cock felt through his jeans and against her ass. Yes, good and hard. And it was totally delicious being bent over, half in and half out of his truck cab in her halter dress, high heels, stockings, garters and thong.

He kissed her bare back, trailing his lips along her spine and sending shivers through her body. Easing his hands into her hair, he pushed it away from the neck of her halter-top and unfastened the clasp. One quick jerk, and he pulled the top of her dress down until her clothing bunched around her waist.

Jake cupped her nipples and she moaned as he fondled them. Her breasts ached and her pussy was so wet for him she could just about scream.

"Let's get in the house," he murmured, his voice a low rumble and his warm breath tickling her back. "I've got to have you."

"Here." Dee pressed her hips back against his cock. "Take me here."

"Don't tempt me." A groan rolled from his throat as he kissed her nape and caressed her breasts. "We need to go inside."

"I *want* you inside. *Me.*" Dee covered his big hands and pressed them tighter to her breasts." "Fuck me *now*, Jake."

"You're incredible." He removed his hands from beneath hers, and she heard the sound of him unfastening his buckle, and then his zipper going down. In the next moment his warm cock pressed against her.

Oh, God. That felt *so* good.

He kneaded and fondled her backside, then trailed his fingers down the crevice. Working his way lower, he teased the curls, but didn't enter the wetness of her pussy.

"You're driving me crazy," Dee murmured as she moved her hips against his hand.

"Good." He slid a finger into her warm pussy, stroking her clit, and Dee dug her nails into the leather upholstery.

"Yes. More," Dee murmured, then gasped when he thrust two fingers inside her.

His strokes intensified. "I love how wet you are for me."

She couldn't wait any longer. She needed to feel him deep inside of her. "Now, baby. *Now.*"

Jake stilled and rested his forehead against the back of her neck. "I don't have a condom."

"There's one at the top of my left stocking."

With a soft chuckle, Jake felt around her stockings until he found the foil package. He slipped it out, and then hooked his fingers around the waist of her thong and eased it down around her thighs.

While he gripped her hips with his hands, he pressed his sheathed cock against her. He teased her with slow thrusts between her legs, but didn't enter her.

Dee clenched her hands in frustration. Bent over like she was, she couldn't reach him—a definite disadvantage. She wanted to be touching him, tasting him.

But did it ever feel incredible. The smell of his leather upholstery surrounded her, along with the scent of cool desert air and sex.

He used both hands to part her pussy lips and pressed his cock against her opening. Oh, thank God. This was what she'd been waiting for. She needed him inside and needed him now.

Dee whimpered and moved her hips back, wanting him to hurry. But he only teased and tortured her, entering a little bit at a time and then pulling back out.

He gripped her hips. "You really want me to fuck you right here?"

"Yes, dammit. Fuck me, Jake!"

With one powerful thrust, he buried his cock inside her. Dee cried out, so close to going over the edge and they'd only started. She'd forgotten how completely he filled her, how fabulous it felt having him inside her.

He plunged in and out, slow and steady.

Too slow.

"Faster, baby. Harder," Dee begged.

In reply he pounded into her, the sound of his flesh slapping against hers filling the night. "You feel nice and tight around me."

"God but you're big." Dee moved her hips back as he thrust into her. "You fuck me so good."

Her breasts chafed against the upholstery as incredible sensations built up inside her. Knowing that she'd need something to hold onto, she reached up and clenched the steering wheel with one hand, while the fingers of her other hand dug into the soft leather seat.

The intensity of her climax took her completely by surprise. It stormed through her like a summer monsoon, and she screamed. Her body rocked against the seat, her orgasm stretching out in endless waves as Jake continued to thrust into her.

And then he growled deep in his throat and shuddered against her backside. She felt his cock pulsating inside her and she pressed against him, wanting to feel every bit of his release.

"Damn, woman." He sank against her back, slipping his hands around her waist and trailing kisses across her shoulders.

"Mmmm," she purred, enjoying the feel of him against her, his cock still inside her. His shirt was soft against her naked back, his jeans coarse against her thighs.

He nuzzled her neck. "After that scream, your dog probably thinks you've been attacked."

Vaguely in the background she heard the sound of Blue barking from inside the house. "I think you might be right."

Jake pulled away and Dee almost whimpered from the feel of his still hard cock leaving her. Taking her by the shoulders, he turned her around, cupped her face in his hands and kissed her.

Oh, could that man kiss.

He moved his lips over hers, gently devouring her in a sensual kiss that turned her body into a mass of melted chocolate, warm and gooey, and ready to pour herself back over him.

When their lips parted, he looked at her and smiled. "Did I mention how incredible you are?"

"Once or twice." Dee kissed the corner of his mouth, fighting the temptation to try for a fourth time. The man probably needed some time to regenerate.

Good Lord, was she becoming a nymph?

Damn straight.

Before she knew what he was doing, he grabbed her around the waist and set her on the front seat of the truck cab, then slid her thong completely off.

"What are you doing?" she asked as he spread her thighs, staring at her mound.

His voice was deep and rough as he replied, "I need to taste you." He hooked her legs over his shoulders and buried his face in her pussy.

"Jake!" Dee cupped her breasts, as he sucked and licked her clit. She squirmed, crying out when he plunged his fingers into her, his satisfied groan against her pussy sending vibrations throughout her.

The leather seat was slick with her sweat as he devoured her, his cheek stubble rough against the sensitive skin of her thighs. She pinched and twisted her nipples, clenching her knees tight around his head. A buzzing filled her mind and she no longer felt anything but his tongue licking her clit, his fingers thrusting inside, and the climax rising within her.

When Dee came, she dug her hands into the leather seat and shouted his name. Jake continued licking her, pushing his face against her until she climaxed yet another time. Her body shuddered with wave after wave of sensation. "Stop! No more!"

Jake pulled back and rested his head on her thigh, a low chuckle coming from him as Dee continued to vibrate beneath him. "Damn, but you taste good, sweetheart," he murmured as he touched her clit with his finger, causing her body to spasm.

"Doooon't," Dee moaned. "I can't take anymore."

"You know what they say about revenge." Jake raised himself up and grabbed Dee's hands, pulling her to a sitting position.

"Revenge?" Her head was still fuzzy from the orgasms.

Pressing her close to him, Jake slowly kissed her. She tasted her own musky scent on his lips. When he raised his head, he smiled. "For that 'down under' experience at the restaurant."

"Oh. That." Dee ran her fingers along the scar that made him seem almost dangerous in the moonlight. "I like your kind of revenge."

After he fastened his belt and jeans, Jake helped Dee straighten her clothes. He closed the door of his truck, wrapped his arm around her shoulders, and walked her to the house.

They started up the steps of her porch, and then he stopped and looked toward the buildings in the back. "Christ, Dee. I forgot about the ranch hands."

"We were on the opposite side of the truck where no one could see." She tugged on his hand and led him up the steps. "Besides, it's Friday night. The guys always head into town, and the bunkhouse isn't even close to the main house, so no one could have seen anything."

Pausing and giving him a mischievous grin, she added, "Not to mention, it made it all the more naughty."

The corner of Jake's mouth turned up and he shook his head. "What am I going to do with you?"

They stopped in front of the door and she gave him a brazen look. "Anything you want."

He placed his hands around her waist and nuzzled the top of her head. "I can think of lots of things."

"Mmmmm. Me, too." Dee reached up and kissed him. She was so tempted to ask him to spend the night, but that wasn't in the plan.

What plan was that again? Oh, yeah. Enjoy the man and let him go when it was time for him to leave.

When she pulled away she unlocked the door, then turned back to him. "Thanks for an unforgettable evening."

Jake glanced at the door and looked like he was about to say something, but then changed his mind.

He cleared his throat. "Ah, I was wondering…"

Dee raised an eyebrow. "Yes?"

"Tomorrow I'm going to my mom's for a couple of hours, for lunch." He ran his hand over the stubble on his cheeks. "Would you like to go?"

Taking a deep breath, she asked, "To meet your mom?"

"Yeah." He put one hand against the doorframe, glanced at his boots and then back to Dee. "Mom can be a bit much to handle in one sitting, though. She's likely to embarrass the hell out of me, and probably you, too."

With a grin Dee slid her arms around his waist. "This I gotta see."

"You'll come then?" He looked both relieved and worried at the same moment.

"Come?" She gave him her most sultry smile. "Is that a promise?"

Jake laughed and kissed her long and hard. "On second thought, it might not be such a great idea. I may not be able to keep my hands off you."

"Sounds like a wonderful idea to me." Dee stepped away and dug her keys out of her purse. "What time?"

"Eleven?"

She unlocked the door. "I'll be waiting."

He kissed her again. "Good night."

"'Night." Dee forced herself to leave his embrace. With one last smile, she slipped in the door and locked it behind her.

Chapter Ten

ॐ

Blue barked, alerting Dee that someone was coming up to the house, just as she finished buttoning her blouse. A sense of mischief came over her as she thought about greeting Jake at the front door, absolutely naked. Yeah, one of these days, she'd have to do exactly that.

Instead, she left the top three buttons undone, just enough to show the red lace bra beneath her lipstick red blouse. She couldn't wait until he got a look at her matching underwear beneath her short jean skirt—that ought to spin his spurs. She dabbed orange blossom perfume between her breasts, at her wrists and behind her knees. Her nipples were already tingling, and her panties wet at the thought of enjoying Jake like she had last night.

A sharp knock sounded. With Blue trotting at her heels, Dee hurried across the tile floor to the front door. Heart racing in anticipation, she flung open the door—but found Kev Grand on her porch, not Jake.

"Heya, Kev." Dee managed to keep the smile on her face and the disappointment out of her voice. "What brings you to the Flying M this morning?"

Kev pushed up the brim of his straw western hat, his hazel eyes traveling over her breasts in a slow perusal. "Now don't you look nice, hon."

Heat singed Dee's cheeks and she barely resisted the urge to button her blouse up to her throat. "I told you I'm not your hon. What's up?"

"I want a word with you." He braced one hand against the doorframe and ran his hand over his mustache and down his stubbled jaw. "I thought you and I were going somewhere with our relationship, but lately, you don't seem too interested."

She caught the smell of chewing tobacco on his breath, but resisted wrinkling her nose. "We've only dated a couple of times." Dee sighed and shook her head. "Where did you get the idea that we'd be anything more than friends? I've never led you on."

"It's Reynolds, isn't it?" Kev clenched his jaw. "He comes into town and you're all over him."

Dee braced her hands on her hips and raised her chin. "I think you've said more than enough."

"Did you ever stop to think that maybe Reynolds has something to do with your missing cattle?" Kev waved toward the rangeland. "Shit started happening not long before he showed up sniffing at your ass."

Anger tinged Dee's vision as crimson as her blouse. "You need to back off right now before you say something that'll *really* piss me off, Kev Grand."

He nodded. "All right. Just don't come crying to me when the bastard dumps you again." As he turned and headed down the steps, he tossed over his shoulder, "Or if you find out he's the one screwing you in more than one way."

Kev's accusation about Jake's involvement with the rustling didn't even dignify a response, as far as Dee was concerned. What an asinine way to try to get her to mistrust Jake.

"Thanks for your concern." Dee glared after Kev as he walked to his appaloosa mare. "So nice of you to be positive I'll get dumped," she added under her breath.

Well, so what if Jake did leave? At least she was getting what she wanted—sex, and damn incredible sex at that.

* * * * *

Jake lowered the visor, blocking out the morning sun as he drove down the dirt road to Dee's ranch. Did she regret what had happened between them last night? All the way home, he'd wavered between wonder at the incredibly erotic evening with her, and berating himself for taking her like he did.

Outside, half in and half out of his truck cab.

Ah, hell. What was the matter with him? Dee deserved better than to be groped in the driveway and then fucked like a teenager in the back of a car. Only they hadn't been in the back at all. He'd had her bent over his truck's leather seats, next to the steering wheel.

As he drove over the cattle guard and up to Dee's house, he spotted a familiar form on horseback, heading across the rangeland.

Grand. Jake gritted his teeth as he shut off the engine. What the hell was Grand doing at Dee's? Again he wondered if the bastard had anything to do with Dee's missing cattle. He'd talked with Forrester and Savage several times over the past couple of weeks, but no decent leads had turned up. The only new information was that damn near every ranch in the area had reported cattle missing.

He scrubbed his hand over his face, and then climbed out of the truck. His steps quickened as he neared the porch and Dee opened the door. Every thought of criminals and cattle dissipated with the breeze as she put her hand on her hip, giving him a smile that made him want to fuck her right there. Her auburn hair hung loose the way he loved it, and she was wearing a red blouse and short jean skirt that hugged her hips, showing her generous curves and long legs.

She cocked her head. "I was beginning to wonder if you were going to stay out in that truck all morning."

In two strides he reached her, slipped his hands around her waist, and kissed her long and hard. "I missed you," he murmured, trailing his lips to her ear. Her orange blossom scent flowed over him, his cock already hard from the feel of her soft body pressed to his.

She gave a husky laugh. "It's only been a few hours."

"Too long." He captured her mouth again, and then with reluctance pulled away.

Dee's mouth was red from his kiss, her nipples pebbled under her blouse. Her breathing came hard and fast. Damn, but he wanted to take her right there in broad daylight on her front porch.

His gaze dropped to the open neck of her blouse and his throat grew tight. She was wearing the heart pendant he'd given her their first Christmas together. Their only Christmas together. He'd chosen the stone because it matched the color of her eyes and it was her birthstone. And he had chosen the shape because she had captured his heart.

He reached up grasped the pendant in his palm. As his gaze met hers, he smiled. "I thought you might have thrown it out in the pasture."

Lips curving into a grin, she gave a throaty laugh. "I gave that some serious consideration."

"I'll bet you did." Jake released the heart and trailed his finger down to the red lace bra peeking out. "Mmmm, I like."

"Wait 'til you see what else I've got on." She gave him a sexy smile and buttoned up her shirt leaving only the top button undone. "Can't go visit your mother with my blouse open."

"Damn, but I preferred it the other way." Jake kissed her again and drew back. "You ready to face lunch with my mom?"

"You make it sound like going in front of a firing squad."

"No, that'd be easier."

She shook her head and laughed again. "Let me grab my purse and say goodbye to Blue."

Jake had only planned to spend a couple of hours with his mom, but that wasn't how it worked out. Dory and Dee had gotten along so well, laughing and joking—mostly at his expense—that they'd ended up staying for hours. Dory had brought out all the embarrassing photos she could find, and told Dee stories Jake had hoped she'd never hear.

By the time he and Dee climbed into his truck to head back to her ranch, it was early evening, starting to get dark.

Dee sat in the middle, next to Jake and buckled her seatbelt. "I like your mom."

"Uh-huh." He slid the key into the ignition and started the truck. "I noticed."

Grinning, she said, "Most fun I've had in a while."

He raised his eyebrows and looked at her. "Yeah?"

She ran her gaze down to his lap and back to his eyes. "Make that the second most fun I've had."

Jake leaned over and kissed her. His stomach rumbled and she gave a soft laugh.

"Hungry?" she murmured against his mouth. "For food, that is."

"Yes on both accounts." He forced himself to pull away from her intoxicating lips. "Want to grab a bite?"

Dee laid her head on his shoulder and sighed. "Why don't we pick up some drive-thru and eat it at my house?"

"All right." His cock was already stirring at the thought of sinking deep inside her.

They went to a fast-food restaurant that served great fried chicken, rolls, mashed potatoes, corn on the cob and jalapeños. The smell of all that food wafted out to the truck and Jake's stomach rumbled even louder.

"Do they have any cheesecake?" Dee asked before he ordered, a wicked glint in her eyes.

Jake's dick grew hard in an instant at the thought of the orgasm she'd had while he fed her chocolate cheesecake. He smiled, his gaze caressing her body, and was rewarded by the sight of her nipples puckering her light blouse.

"You and cheesecake are a dangerous combination," he murmured.

After Dee let Blue out into the night to do his business, she joined Jake in the dining room where he'd spread out all the food on the long oak table. Smells of fried chicken and mashed potatoes filled the room and her stomach growled. He'd taken a couple of plates from the china cabinet and silverware from the buffet. It surprised her that he remembered where everything was kept after all these years.

The chandelier was on, the crystals casting rainbows of light around the room. Jake sat at the end of the table. She took the seat next to him, and dug into the meal.

In minutes, he finished eating another chicken breast and tossed the bones into the growing pile. "I'll help you with chores since we're late getting back."

Dee shook her head. "My foreman said he'd take care of everything today. I asked Jess this morning since I didn't know how long you and I would be gone."

"How long has Lawless worked for you?" Jake asked in between bites of mashed potatoes and gravy.

"A couple of months now." She spied a roll and grabbed it. "He was referred to me by a friend of Steve Wilds."

Jake nodded. "Wilds is a rancher?"

"Yeah." Dee sipped her soda. "You know him?"

"I've run into him a couple of times."

"Catie is his sister." Dee jerked her thumb north. "They own the ranch on that side of the Flying M. So far they've been lucky enough not to lose any cattle. Which is odd since pretty much everyone else has."

She polished off a wing and discarded the bones. As she licked the remaining juice from her fingers, she glanced up and her eyes met Jake's. He was watching her with a look that was akin to a man in desperate need. Slowly and deliberately she sucked each finger, never letting her gaze waver from his.

With a groan, he stood and drew her up with him. "You're driving me out of my ever-lovin' mind."

"Am I?" She feigned innocence as she watched him from beneath her lashes, her eyes on his mouth.

"Uh-huh." In a quick motion he shoved their plates and food containers to the middle of the table, and pulled the chair away from the end. "It's time for dessert."

Before she knew what was happening, he grabbed her around the waist, lifted her up and placed her on top of the table. He stepped between her thighs and cupped her face with his hands. But he made no move to kiss her, just smiled and traced his thumb along her lower lip.

Her body quivered and she couldn't take her eyes off his mouth and the cleft in his chin. "Am I dessert?"

"Most definitely."

Wrapping her arms around his neck, she pulled his mouth toward hers. "Kiss me."

She felt his smile against her lips and he gave her an achingly slow kiss. Too slow. She wanted him in the worst way, yet she held back from plunging her tongue into his mouth, letting him set the pace. He smelled so good, so musky, so male.

"Every time I had dinner with your family at this table," he whispered as he lifted his head, "I fantasized about fucking you on top of it."

"You did?"

"Uh-huh."

God, how that made her hot and wet.

His hungry mouth moved to her earlobe and she gasped as he nipped at it. "Right underneath this chandelier. I'd picture you naked, wearing only that heart necklace."

Shivers raced through Dee as he slipped his hands into her hair and slid his tongue into her mouth. He tasted spicy and wild, and she couldn't get enough of him.

Dee pulled Jake's black T-shirt out of the waistband of his jeans. "Now, baby. I want you to fuck me now."

Jake captured her hands in his, and then kissed her knuckles. "Let's take it a little slower this time." He put her hands in her lap and started unbuttoning her blouse.

She whimpered in frustration, but let him take control.

It seemed to take him forever to get to the last button. "Now in my fantasy, you're sitting here completely naked, just waiting for me."

He pushed her blouse off her shoulders and down her arms, then tossed it onto a chair. The air felt cool on Dee's exposed skin, and she quivered with anticipation.

Cupping her breasts with his palms, Jake ran his thumbs over the lace bra covering her, and she moaned. He moved his hands to the front clasp and undid it, releasing her aching breasts.

After Jake slid the bra off and tossed it aside, he didn't touch her pussy like she was dying for him to do. Instead, he crouched down to remove her shoes. When he finished, he stood and unbuttoned her skirt, the touch of his hands against her belly burning her like wildfire. She leaned back, bracing her palms on the table and lifting her hips so that he could slide the skirt off.

When he'd dropped them to the floor, he moved between her thighs and pressed himself against the crotch of her lace panties. His jeans felt rough and erotic against the insides of her thighs, and he felt so damn hard against her.

"God, you're sexy." He moved back and traced a finger down the damp center of her pussy. "And so wet for me."

Just that light touch almost made her come. Dee's breathing grew heavier, her heart pounding in her throat. She wanted to beg him to fuck her, yet she was so incredibly aroused by what he was doing.

The table felt cool and smooth to her naked bottom as he eased her panties over her hips. He tossed them over his shoulder, then pushed her thighs apart. But still he didn't touch her pussy, just stepped back and raked his gaze over her body. She was completely naked with only her heart pendant on, and he was fully clothed. She'd never been so turned on.

The chandelier cast rainbows of light across her breasts and her nipples grew impossibly harder as he studied her. His gray eyes were smoky, his gaze filled with such intense heat that her skin burned wherever it rested.

She felt raw and exposed. The slightest movement of air brushing across her skin just about made her scream.

"I want to watch you touch yourself." Jake's voice was rough.

Dee swallowed, her eyes widening and her lips parting.

"That's part of my fantasy," he murmured. "Touch yourself."

She moved her hands to her breasts, keeping her eyes focused on his and ran the tip of her tongue along her lower lip.

Jake groaned and clenched his fists at his sides, his erection straining against his jeans. "Move one hand lower."

The fact that he was obviously as turned on as she was, gave Dee the courage to shed her inhibitions. If he wanted a show, she'd give it to him.

She eased one hand from her breast, down her belly, closer to her thighs.

"Yes. Lower." He groaned again. "Tease your pussy."

She parted her thighs even wider and reached the curls below. Jake looked like he was in mortal pain as she slid her finger into her hot center. She was so wet. So hot for him. With her other hand she continued to knead her breast while she stroked her clit, widening her legs so he could see her dampness. Smell her desire.

His Adam's apple bobbed as he swallowed hard. "Lick your nipple."

Dee stilled for a second, but the lust in his eyes made her wonder if her breasts were large enough to comply. Her eyes still locked with his, she lifted her breast and bent her head down to flick her tongue over her own nipple while still stroking herself. With him watching her, the feeling was so erotic that she nearly reached climax.

His next words came out in a growl, "Come for me, Dee."

Dee's eyes widened. Her fingers slowed for a moment, and her cheeks burned. But Jake's eyes. Oh, God. He was fucking her with his eyes, watching each slow circle as she rubbed herself.

"Yes," he whispered as she picked up speed again, barely able to keep her eyes open.

"Come for me, sweetheart." Jake's voice was a low hum, driving her forward.

She bit her lip to hold back cries of pleasure, then couldn't. Her breath came in quick gasps as she rubbed harder and harder.

"Now," he demanded. "Right now!"

Jake's command threw her off the summit and she came in an explosive orgasm that rocked her from head to toe.

In the next moment he stood between her thighs, his mouth taking possession of hers. He held her tight in his arms as her body shuddered.

Jake released her mouth to move downward, capturing between his teeth the nipple she'd licked for him. Aftershocks racked Dee's body and she arched to meet him, sliding her hands into his thick black hair.

"You're so perfect," he murmured as he moved to the other peak and then nipped at it.

More cries escaped Dee's throat as she clenched her hands in his hair while he suckled and licked her nipples. "I can't wait, anymore. I need you inside me."

When she tugged at his T-shirt, this time he helped her. He ripped it the rest of the way off and threw it to the floor before gripping her hips.

Dee slid her hands through his chest hair, loving the feel of his muscles against her sensitive fingertips. She continued down his taut abdomen to the V of hair that disappeared into his jeans.

Shaking with desire, she undid his belt and the top button. As she slid his zipper down, she pulled away his briefs and sighed as she released the full length of his cock.

Her mouth watered as she caressed his rod, feeling his thickness in her hand. So hard, yet soft all at the same time.

Jake groaned as she ran her thumb over the head, brushing the pearly bead of semen at the tip, and was gratified by his sharp intake of breath.

Her gaze met his, and he groaned again as she brought her thumb to her mouth and licked the salty sweetness of his semen. "You taste so good."

He pushed his jeans and briefs around his thighs. After whipping on protection, he slid his finger into the creamy wetness of her pussy.

"Now, baby." She strained closer to him, gripping his bare shoulders and hooking her thighs around his hips.

Jake pressed the tip of his erection against the swollen flesh between her thighs, his gaze locked with hers.

She braced her arms on the table and bucked her hips. "Fuck me, dammit!"

In tune with her desire, Jake plunged his cock into her, burying himself as deep as he could go.

Grasping her hips tighter, he took her hard and fast. Dee's breasts bounced with every thrust as she clenched him between her thighs, her head back and her lips parted.

It felt so good having him pounding inside. "Yes," she cried. "Harder. Faster. *Harder*!"

She twisted and screamed as another violent orgasm seized her.

"Dee…" Jake thrust into her a few more times and then shouted her name again as he shuddered with his own climax. He clenched her hips as he pulsated inside her his cock throbbing and jerking as his semen spilled inside her.

Bracing his arms on either side of Dee, Jake leaned forward and pressed his forehead against hers. His breathing was heavy, his sweat mingling with hers, the smell of sex surrounding them.

Jake's smile matched Dee's, and as he kissed her she felt him harden inside her. She almost groaned in frustration when he withdrew, still partially erect.

Cupping her breast, he caressed her nipple with his thumb, sending more shivers through her. "Thanks for making a man's fantasy come true."

Dee smiled and trailed kisses along his scar to the corner of his mouth. "Anytime, cowboy."

"I'll hold you to that." He held her close to him, as though he never wanted to let her go.

And Dee was afraid she never wanted him to.

Jake could hardly believe how completely Dee had fulfilled his fantasy of watching her masturbate, and of fucking her on top of the table. If he hadn't shot his load three times last night, he was sure he would have come in his jeans while he watched her bring herself to climax.

When he could finally bring himself to step away from her, he pulled his jeans up around his hips and helped her off the table.

Dee leaned against him. "Hold me," she murmured against his chest. "My legs are too wobbly after that round of Earth shattering sex."

"Earth shattering, huh?" He nibbled her earlobe, amazed at how hard he was again. "Let's go for exploding universe sex next."

She shivered as his tongue dipped into her ear. "Does that have anything to do with the big bang theory?"

Jake chuckled. God, she was wonderful. "Why don't we find out?"

"You're on." Dee leaned more fully against him. "But first let me get my legs working again."

"I can take care of that."

Dee squealed and clung to him as he scooped her up in his arms. Holding her close, he carried her down the long hallway to her room, his boots echoing against the tile in the silent house. He remembered exactly where her room was, as though he'd been there yesterday. He'd never fucked her in her home before, much less her bedroom, but when no one was around they had shared more than a few kisses in there.

Light spilled into the dark bedroom from the hallway, illuminating a huge bed in the center of her room. A snowy comforter covered it, matching pillows and bolsters piled near the brass headboard.

Just as Jake laid Dee on the bed and stepped back to start to remove his jeans, Blue's barking caught his attention. Blue carried on, growling and snarling outside Dee's window.

"Something—or someone—is out there." Dee's hushed voice filled Jake with concern. "Blue never barks like that unless there's a reason."

"Keep the light off." A mixture of rage and wariness gave Jake a surge of strength. He moved away from her, wishing he hadn't left his gun in his truck. He eased to one of the room's windows and lifted the curtain with his finger, just enough to look out into the starlit night.

When Jake's eyes adjusted to the darkness of the night, he saw Blue a few feet from the window. The dog's hackles were practically standing on edge as he continued to growl and bark in the direction of the barn—but at what?

Jake heard the rustle of fabric as Dee moved behind him, then saw out of the corner of his eye that she had slid on a robe. "See anything?" she whispered.

"No—" he started to reply, just as a shadowed figure eased from the black mouth of the barn, moving slowly in the shadows. "Damn."

Without a second thought, Jake whirled and sprinted from Dee's bedroom toward the front door. "Stay in the house," he called over his shoulder as he hurried.

"Jake! Dammit…" Her feet padded against the floor as she followed him down the hallway. "You'd better be careful."

With stealth that came naturally to him, enhanced by years of work in law enforcement, Jake silently opened the front door and slipped onto the porch and into the night. Blue still barked, sparing Jake only a quick glance before growling again at the shadows around the barn.

Jake's heart rate picked up as he neared his truck, planning to grab his gun from beneath the seat. The night air chilled his bare chest, but he barely noticed. The fire of pursuit burned in his blood.

Just as he reached his truck door, he saw the shadow sprint from the barn into the nearby mesquite bushes. Jake yanked the door open and grabbed his weapon, then took off across the yard toward the barn. The sound of a horse's whinny followed by hoof beats told him he was too late.

In the distance he saw the shadowy outline of a horse and rider heading toward the mountains.

Jake knew he'd never catch up to them, so instead he gripped his gun and eased out to the barn. When he was sure he was alone, he flipped on the barn light and searched the place. The only thing he found amiss was the latch to Imp's stall undone, but thank God the little bastard of a calf was still there.

Chapter Eleven

પ્ય

Settling back in a chair in the breakfast nook, Jake took a swig of the beer Dee had given him while he watched her pace the kitchen floor. He'd made the proper calls to all the proper departments. Jarrod Savage and his deputy were on their way.

"Why would somebody trespass and hang around my barn?" Dee hugged her arms beneath her breasts as she moved, the motion plumping them up so that they almost spilled out of the opening of the blouse she was now wearing. "And why did they mess with Imp's stall?"

Jake's cock twitched as he watched her. Damn, but it had been only an hour since he'd taken her on the tabletop, and he was raring for more. Too bad they'd have to wait for Savage to do his dog-and-pony show.

But the thought of someone being on Dee's property cooled his lust. He cursed himself for thinking about sex when he should be figuring out who was responsible for the rustling, and who had tried to steal Dee's calf. Mentally he ran down the list of suspects and motives as Dee paced.

Kev Grand had a real thing for her—maybe he was trying to get some kind of sick revenge for Dee pushing off his advances. Jake was still irked about Kev's accusation— Dee had told him about it while they waited for the sheriff. Why would Kev try to throw suspicion on Jake?

Then there was that new foreman, Jess Lawless. Something about the man didn't quite fit, and it was pissing Jake off not being able to place what it was. Come Monday at work, he'd have to do a little research.

Of the other neighboring ranchers, so far Steve Wilds was the only one who hadn't had any cattle stolen. From what Jake had heard from Deputy Forrester, the Wilds were hard up for cash. But it was a little too obvious and a little too stupid to not take his own.

Outside Blue barked, and Jake heard the sound of a vehicle driving up. Looked like it was time to see what the sheriff had to say.

Dee's stomach was in knots as she and Jake headed outside to meet the sheriff. Savage had made it there faster than she'd expected. He was the sheriff for all of Cochise County, and his office was a good thirty minute drive from her ranch. He must have been in the area when Jake made the call.

When she could make out the sheriff's features in the porch light, she saw that he was one cool drink of water. He'd only recently been elected, and she hadn't had the opportunity to meet him before. The man was at least six feet tall, broad shouldered and muscular. And when he took off his tan Stetson, she noticed he had the most amazing crystal green eyes to go along with his thick brown hair and sable mustache.

"Dean MacLeod," Dee said as she held out her hand to shake the sheriff's. She couldn't help but think that Catie's panties would be in a twist if she got a look at this fine cowboy. "It's a pleasure to meet you, Sheriff."

"Jarrod Savage." The man had a deep rumbling voice that had to turn on every woman he met. He smiled as he took her hand. "Pleasure's all mine."

The sheriff released Dee's hand and turned to Jake. "Good to see you again, partner, although I'm not partial to the circumstances."

Jake took Dee's hand and started toward the barn. "Where's Forrester?" he asked.

Savage fell into step beside them. "Deputy Forrester checked in too far away to respond to the call." His voice had a slightly annoyed note to it. "His instructions were to stay in this area, but he was chasing a lead to the south. He has the damn department's horse trailer, too."

As they walked to the barn, Jake explained what had happened in detail that amazed Dee. How he saw and remembered so much in just that brief amount of time gave Dee added respect for his profession.

A cool breeze swept over Dee's skin and she shivered. Jake casually wrapped one arm around her shoulders and held her close, warming her, even as he continued talking with Savage.

The sheriff lifted a partial print off the latch to Imp's stall. "Likely it was a close-by job since the perp was on horseback," Savage said when he finished taking the evidence.

Jake nodded, his arm still tight around Dee. "Hard to imagine it could be connected to the rustling."

Savage gave an ironic smile. "But you sure as hell never know."

"Ain't that the truth." Jake kept Dee close as they headed back to the house. "Come daylight I'll be cutting sign."

"Say what?" Dee looked from Savage to Jake.

Jake brushed his lips over her hair. "Lingo for following the tracks of the bastard."

When they reached the Sheriff's truck, they said their goodbyes, Savage promising to follow up with them in the next couple of days.

After they'd taken a shower together and had eaten a light supper, Jake scooped Dee up and carried her to the bedroom. In the distance he heard the sound of thunder, and a gust of wind rattled the panes of her bedroom window.

He laid Dee on the bed and for endless seconds he just stood and looked at her. The robe had fallen completely open, and beneath it she was wearing only the peridot heart pendant and had never looked more gorgeous than she did at that moment.

Those clear green eyes were wide, drinking him in the same way he was watching her. Her hair spread out like wildfire against the white comforter, her lips red and swollen, her nipples hard and dark. His gaze slid over her porcelain skin, the sprinkling of freckles across her one bared shoulder and on down to that patch of auburn curls on the mound between her firm thighs.

"You're so beautiful, I can barely breathe," he whispered.

"Come to me, Jake." Her voice was a caress and a demand all in one.

When he had shed his boots and the last bit of his clothing, he eased onto the bed next to Dee.

Jake helped her completely remove the robe, and then propped himself up on one elbow. He had to struggle not to climb between her thighs and fuck her hard and fast again.

No, this time he wanted to make love to her, and cherish every bit of her body.

He smiled and allowed himself to caress her cheek. An overwhelming urge came over him, to tell her those three words lodged in his heart and soul.

I love you.

No. It was too soon. He had to win her trust and her love again. There was no doubt in his mind that she was his—he just had to take it a little slower this time to convince her.

Instead of uttering the words he longed to say, he brushed his lips over hers. She sighed, her warm breath fanning over his mouth. He ran his tongue along her lower lip, then caught it gently between his teeth and caressed the captured flesh with his tongue.

Soft cries rose from her throat as he released her lip and delved into the warm recesses of her mouth. He dipped his tongue inside, tasting her like a hummingbird drinking nectar from a blossom.

As Jake kissed Dee, he trailed his fingers down her shoulder and arm to her waist and over the curve of one hip. His fingers skimmed her flesh, light brushes that caused her to shiver and goose bumps to roughen her soft skin.

In turn she stroked him, her nails lightly raking his hips and thighs and his back. Her touch was harder than his, as if understanding that his male skin required a firmer touch than her softer femininity.

"Make love to me," she murmured as her hand slid up his back and into his hair.

"I am, sweetheart."

Slowly Jake kissed and explored every part of her body he could reach, using his lips and tongue and hands. Dee's hands continued to stroke his muscles and his cock as he kissed the tender spot below her earlobe, then moved to the hollow at the base of her throat where her hand always crept when she was nervous. His tongue found the soft skin of her shoulder, the mole above her breast, the curve of her waist and her navel.

Lower and lower he worked downward until he reached the auburn curls between her thighs. He nuzzled the soft hair of her pussy and drank in the scent of her arousal.

Jake looked up to see her watching him, her eyes dark with passion, her chest rising and falling.

He kept his eyes focused on her pussy as his tongue dipped into her pussy and he tasted her. Her eyes widened and her body jerked at the contact.

"Jake." His name was a plea and a promise on her lips.

Sliding two fingers inside of her warm core, he moved his mouth over her pussy, licking her clit and enjoying her taste.

And when her body tensed, he slipped his hands under her hips and pressed his mouth harder against her pussy, driving her mercilessly toward completion. Her body arched up off the bed and she cried out as her orgasm tore through her.

Even then, he didn't stop. "Jake. Baby," she moaned. But then she was too helpless to do anything more than ride the next wave sweeping through her.

Rain pattered on the windowpane, a distant sound that somehow made their joining even more intimate.

Before she had completely come down from the summit, Jake rose above Dee and thrust his sheathed cock into her. He fought for control as he took her slow and easy, reveling in the sensation of being inside her core and wanting to prolong it as long as possible.

Dee wrapped her legs around his waist, her hands clenching his hips, her eyes closed.

"Look at me." Jake's voice came out in a rough growl. "Watch me fuck you."

She opened her eyes, her gaze meeting his, and he couldn't hold back any longer. He pounded into her, like the rain that was now pounding down on the house. She begged him for more, urging him on, like parched earth begging for moisture.

Jake shouted Dee's name as he climaxed, buried so deep inside her that he never wanted to find his way back.

Tempting aromas teased Jake's nose. He blinked away the light and realized he was alone in Dee's bed, and it was morning.

Mentally he cursed himself for not following the tracks as soon as the sheriff had taken off. After last night's storm, it was likely there wasn't a damn thing left to track. Jake had been more interested in fucking than following up on what might have been their first real lead. After all, he was Customs and more experienced at cutting sign than Savage was.

Through the open bedroom door came the delicious scents of coffee, sausage and eggs, and if he wasn't mistaken, maple syrup. His stomach, surely tired of dry cornflakes and milk every morning, growled its loud demand for the food he smelled.

He climbed out of bed and pulled on his briefs and jeans, then padded barefoot and shirtless down the cool ceramic tile to the kitchen. The sizzle of sausages and clanking of plates met him as he rounded the corner and saw Dee.

She stood in front of the huge stainless steel range top, using a spatula to scoop a pancake from the griddle and then flipping it onto a plate.

For a moment he leaned against the doorway and just watched her as she poured more batter onto the griddle and then set the bowl down. She scooped sausages out of another pan and onto a plate, then turned the burner off beneath the frying pan.

Her long auburn hair hung wild and loose down her back, and if he wasn't mistaken she was wearing his black T-shirt. It came to mid-thigh on her, and her legs and feet were bare.

A lump formed in Jake's throat at the homey image Dee made as she cooked breakfast. What would it be like to wake up with her every morning? Having her beside him for conversation over pancakes and coffee. Being with her after work and sharing what had happened in each of their days. And to have her to hold in his arms every night.

Dee glanced over her shoulder and greeted him with a grin that warmed his blood and made his cock rise. "'Bout time you got up, cowboy."

Smiling, Jake walked across the floor. When he reached her, he slid his arms around her waist and hugged her from behind, nuzzling her ear. "Mornin'."

She sighed and leaned back against him. "Hungry?"

"Starving." He nipped at her ear and moved to the curve of her neck. "Everything smells wonderful. Including you."

With a soft laugh, she replied, "This pancake is going to be burnt to a crisp if you don't stop messing with the cook."

"Small price to pay," he murmured. But he stepped back, releasing his hold on her. For now.

He shoved his hands in his front pockets and leaned over the plates of pancakes, sausages and scrambled eggs, sniffing with the appreciation of a starving male.

"Done." Dee flipped the last pancake onto the stack and turned the burner's heat off. "Now if you'll help me carry these to the breakfast nook, you can dig in."

Jake took his hands from his pockets and picked up the plates of pancakes and sausages. "Your every desire is my command," he said as he headed to the round oak table near the bay window.

"That's what I'm counting on." Her tone was sultry and teasing, and damned if it didn't make his cock even harder.

He set the food in the middle of the table, which was already set with plates, flatware and napkins. He went back to the counter and picked up the dish of scrambled eggs and the pot of coffee.

Dee grabbed a glass carafe of orange juice from the fridge. She stopped to retrieve the saucepan of maple syrup that had been heating on the range top, and then joined him at the table.

"Oh, the cream." She jumped back up and went to the fridge. Jake watched her as she bent over to search the lower shelves, his T-shirt hiking up over her hips and exposing her bottom.

She wasn't wearing any underwear.

Jake's mouth fell open as he stared at the exposed pink folds of her pussy, and he wondered what refrigerator sex would be like.

Ice-cold air blowing over their naked bodies as he bent her over in the open door of the fridge. Dee clutching the shelves that held milk and eggs, her nipples hard from the chill. Her screams of pleasure as she yelled at him to fuck her harder while he thrust his cock deep inside her.

"Found it." She stood and turned, holding the small crystal pitcher of cream, then shut the fridge door with a bump of her hip.

"Aren't you hungry?" She frowned as she came back to the table and sat. "You haven't touched a thing."

He cleared his throat. "Ah, just waiting for you."

She rewarded him with a smile and poured two cups of coffee. "So, my cowboy prince is a gentleman, too."

"I wouldn't say that," he muttered as he added a touch of cream to his coffee. He piled pancakes on his plate and slathered them with butter and warm maple syrup. "What are your plans for the day?" he asked as he speared a couple of sausages.

Dee was just about to take a bite of pancake. Pausing, she held her fork in midair and shrugged. "I haven't made any."

He shoveled scrambled eggs on the last remaining spot on his plate. "Why don't we spend the day together?"

With a smile that reached her beautiful green eyes, she replied, "I'd like that."

Relief flooded through him, and his muscles relaxed. A part of him had been afraid she wouldn't want to spend the rest of the weekend with him.

Dee chewed her mouthful of pancake then chased it down with a drink of orange juice. "Why don't we go horseback riding in the canyon?"

Jake swallowed the bite of sausage he was eating and gave her a slow grin. "Up to our place?"

"Yes." The way she was looking at him when she said it made him wonder how he managed to control himself from taking her on the kitchen table. Right here and now.

He downed his orange juice before asking, "When is your sister coming for a visit?"

"Not until December."

"Need any help with chores?"

"Nah." Dee smiled. "I told you yesterday that Jess will make sure it's taken care of."

Jake just nodded. Something about Dee's foreman just didn't fit. Lawless moved and worked like a professional cow hand, but Jake's law enforcement gut told him there was more to Lawless than outward appearances. Jake's instinct wasn't clear on whether to trust the man or not.

And if he should consider Lawless as competition for Dee's affection. Or was that just fouling Jake's radar, and making him suspect an innocent man? He had no hard proof of anything, save Jess not giving Dee that one message.

Jake and Dee ate the rest of their breakfast in companionable silence. After eating, they both cleaned and loaded the dishwasher.

When they finished, he captured her around the waist and lifted her onto the polished granite surface of the kitchen island.

She laughed, her eyes sparkling, and moistened her lips with the tip of her tongue. "What do you think you're doing, Jake Reynolds?"

"Having brunch." He brushed his lips over hers. "And this is just the right height."

Dee shivered. "I never knew granite could feel so cool and delicious against my skin."

Trailing his thumb over her bottom lip, Jake said, "Especially when you're not wearing any underwear?"

She cradled his jaw with one hand, stroking his stubble with her thumb. "How did you know that?"

"Lucky guess?"

"Uh-huh."

Dee pulled him toward her and demanded entrance to his mouth. Her fingertips skated over his nipples, running through the hair on his chest, and working on down to the button of his jeans.

He slid his hands onto her bare ass, pushing the T-shirt up as he pressed his jean-clad cock against her pussy.

"Hey, Dean?" a masculine voice shouted from the direction of the front door.

Dee jerked her head up and yelped. She attempted to scramble down from the island, but Jake kept her butt pinned to the granite countertop.

While Dee tried to tug the T-shirt lower to cover herself, Jake looked over his shoulder and called out, "In the kitchen."

"I found—" Jess Lawless started to say, but came to an abrupt stop when he saw Jake and Dee. "Jeez. Sorry, Dean. Didn't mean to disturb you two." The ranch foreman looked more amused than embarrassed at having come across his boss half-clothed and in the arms of an almost naked man. "Howdy, Reynolds."

"Mornin', Lawless," Jake said, but made it clear by his territorial stance that Dee was his woman.

Dee cleared her throat, and when Jake glanced at her he noticed the pink in her cheeks. "Can this wait, Jess?"

"Sure thing." The ranch hand nodded. "Just wanted to let you know I ran across another downed fence. This time along the Wilds' side of the ranch."

"Damn." Dee pushed her loose hair over her shoulder. "You and the boys have it taken care of?"

"You bet."

Lawless started to turn around, but stopped when Jake said, "Someone was prowling around the barn last night. Did you see anything?"

The ranch hand paused and frowned. "No. You?"

Jake related what had happened, watching Lawless as he spoke. But the man revealed nothing in his expression.

When Jake finished, Lawless said, "I'll check it out and see if anything's missing or disturbed." He nodded to Jake and then to Dee. "Catch you later."

Jake narrowed his eyes as he watched the foreman leave. He was definitely going to have to do a little research on one Jess Lawless.

Dee's thoughts were wild with confusion. The night she had shared with Jake, the intruder on her property, Jess's announcement that the fence was down—sheesh. All she wanted to think about was the fabulous sex she'd enjoyed with Jake, but the strange happenings kept tugging at her.

After they showered, dressed, packed a lunch and saddled a pair of horses, Jake and Dee headed to the mountain behind the Flying M ranch. The morning smelled crisp and clean, of rain-washed sky, wet earth and grass. Dee wore a light jacket, a T-shirt with no bra, and loose cotton slacks with no underwear. She was damn good and prepared to enjoy Jake there and back again.

On their way, they stopped and checked out the fence line that had been cut over night. Her efficient cowhands had already repaired the fence, boot prints, horse hooves and cow tracks all mixed up in the muddy ground so that there was no easy way to identify any one print.

When they continued on to the hideout and guided their horses deeper into the canyon, Dee vibrated with desire for Jake. Every nerve in her body was aware and alive with need, screaming for his touch, his mouth, his body. Crying out for his cock to be deep inside her. When they were out of sight of the ranch, she reined in Shadow.

Jake pulled up Whisper. "What? We're not going to our place?"

She slid off her jacket while she studied him from beneath her lashes. "Remember how we fulfilled your fantasy yesterday?"

"Yeah." His gray eyes positively smoldered, and she knew he was thinking of that moment when he asked her to make herself come. And then how she'd done it.

As she tied her jacket to the pummel of her saddle, she licked her lips. "I've always fantasized about riding double."

He gazed at her for a long moment, taking her in from the nipples jutting against her blouse, down to where the cotton slacks hid her pussy. Without another word, he swung down from Whisper and tied the lead reins to the back of Dee's saddle. He mounted Shadow, sliding into the saddle behind Dee, his hips glued to hers.

His erection was positively enormous. Dee sank back against him and wiggled her ass against his cock. "I wish we were naked," she murmured.

Jake slid his arms around her waist and nibbled at her neck. "That can be arranged."

With a soft laugh, Dee guided her gelding through the trees, Jake's mare following behind. Rainwater slid from the leaves as they passed through the trees, lightly showering Dee and Jake with moisture. Their bodies moved together with the gentle walk of the horse, Jake's cock growing harder against Dee's backside, increasing the ache in her pussy.

He kissed the back of her neck, using his tongue and lips to drive her wild. "Tell me about this fantasy."

Dee was so hot and so wet for him. "In my fantasy, you're a desperado and you've kidnapped me off my horse. You're taking me to your hideout to ravish me."

Jake's soft laugh tickled her skin. "And you're the *señorita* in distress with no one to rescue you."

She whimpered. "Touch me, baby."

"Where do you want my hands?" His voice was a deep growl against her nape. "Tell me. Exactly what you want."

Dee was so turned on that she was barely able to keep her eyes open to guide Shadow along the trail. "I want you to unbutton my shirt and let the breeze caress my breasts."

He eased his hands across her, stroking her sensitive nipples through the material. Slowly he unbuttoned her blouse until it gaped open.

The intense sensation of cool air on her naked breasts caused Dee to gasp. Her nipples beaded, begging for Jake's touch. His calloused fingers trailed lazy circles around her heart pendant and across her bare skin, but avoided where she ached to be touched the most.

"Jake," she moaned.

He lightly bit her neck and tickled the flesh with his tongue. "What do you want me to do next?"

Dee swallowed and licked her lips. "I want your hands to play with my nipples."

A few more circles around her breasts and then his fingers found her tight peaks. At first he just brushed them, teasing her with the light caress.

She pressed back against him and moaned as he cupped her breasts in his large palms. Then he took her nipples between his thumbs and forefingers, pulling and kneading them. Dee moved her hips against his cock, in time with Shadow's gait, wanting the release that only Jake could give her.

"Is that all?" His mouth continued to kiss her neck and her ear, and she shivered from the exquisite sensations coursing through her.

"No." She knew he was going to make her tell him, and then he'd give her what she wanted. "Make me come."

He sucked in his breath and she could tell he was as aroused as she was. If it was physically possible, she would have turned around to go down on his cock while they were on horseback, taking him to the back of her throat.

The clip clop sound of Whisper's and Shadow's hooves kept time with the beating of Dee's heart. Smells of horse, leather, and piñon filled the air, and Jake's musky scent surrounded her. A breeze rushed through the trees, a sensual murmur and a whisper in her soul.

The horse moved between her thighs, the rocking motion increasing the ache in her pussy as Jake's hands stroked her skin from her breasts to her waist. He eased one hand down to her crotch, and Dee gasped as he cupped her mound, then rubbed at her through the thin cotton material. She would have given anything to be wearing absolutely nothing at that moment.

"Touch me." She was begging, needing him so bad she couldn't stand it any longer.

Jake eased his hand under the elastic waistband of her baggy slacks, pausing to tease the curls of her pussy with his fingers. His breathing became as ragged as hers. "God, but it turns me on when you're naked beneath your clothes."

Dee barely had the presence of mind to guide Shadow to the right and onto the trail that would take them to their secluded spot. Her body was on fire, and she wished she could take Jake's cock deep within her right then. "Now, Jake."

He chuckled close to her ear, sending shivers through her and making her ache even more. He slid his fingers deeper into her slacks, delving into her wetness. She gasped as he stroked her, caressed her, circling her sensitive clit.

Dee clenched the reins as he drove her on until she reached the summit and climaxed, her orgasm splintering throughout her body. She cried out with her release, causing Shadow to shy and toss his head.

Her body jerked against Jake's hand, but he still didn't let up. Aftershocks rippled throughout her body, one after another, until finally she begged him to stop.

The intensity of her orgasm made her completely boneless, and she melted against Jake. He trailed kisses from her hair to her ear while the horse headed through the trees. Dee sighed, absolute contentment warming her body as he wrapped his arms around her.

He nipped at her earlobe. "We're almost there."

"When we get to our spot, I'm going to give you the best orgasm of your life, Jake Reynolds."

"I'm ready." His fingers played with her nipples, and his cock was oh-so-hard against her ass.

Oh, yes. That man was ready.

"Good," she murmured. "And when we're finished, I'm going to make you come again."

Chapter Twelve

ఐ

He felt like he'd come home.

"It's just as beautiful here as I'd remembered," Jake murmured when they arrived in the small canyon, their hidden spot.

Oak and piñon trees filled the secluded area. Starting from high in the canyon, a rain-swollen stream gurgled and bubbled through a series of boulders down a small incline. Dee reined in the gelding beside the stream, and Jake's mare came to a stop behind them.

Wave after wave of memories flowed over him as he held Dee, touching the soft skin he'd bared. This was where they'd made love the first time, and many more after that. They'd shared hopes and dreams for the future—a future she'd once thought included him. Whether she knew it or not, he intended to be a part of her dreams again.

"Better get me down before I let you ravish me on horseback," Dee murmured.

"Mmmm. I like the sound of that." Jake slid Dee's blouse off her shoulders and pulled it away, leaving her naked from the waist up.

Dee gasped and shivered. He slid his hands down her arms, feeling the goose bumps that had broken out from the contact of cool air against her skin.

Shadow swished his tail and stomped a hoof, but stood patiently as Jake caressed Dee's bare flesh.

"Take off your shirt," she demanded.

Jake put his hat on Dee, pulled off his own T-shirt, and then tossed it and her blouse onto a boulder near the stream. He put his hat back on his head as she sighed and leaned against him, her hair like silk against his naked chest. His own nipples hardened, and he throbbed with the need to fuck her with everything he had.

He moved his mouth close to her ear. "Put one leg over so that you're sitting sidesaddle."

With Jake's help, Dee brought her leg over, and then she was sideways in his lap, her arms around his neck. She looked up at him, her eyes wide and that beautiful green that he knew he could get lost in.

"*Now*, I'm going to ravish you." He leaned down to caress her mouth with his, slowly tasting her. God, he would never get enough of this woman.

His woman.

Dee made soft little moans as he thrust into her mouth. He ran his tongue inside of her lips and along the serrated edge of her teeth. His chest brushed her breasts as he pressed her close and his ache for her increased.

Trailing kisses from her mouth, over her chin, to the hollow of her throat and past her neck, Jake worked his way down to Dee's breasts. He licked around her heart pendant, her orange blossom scent filling his senses, as his tongue tasted the salty flavor of her skin.

They rocked as Shadow shifted beneath them and swatted his tail again.

"Jake," Dee cried out when his mouth found its treasure, her hard, rosy nipple. "I want you inside me so bad."

He groaned, wanting to slide between her thighs and fuck her fast and hard. But instead, he lowered his voice and said, "As soon as I have my way with you."

"Have your way with me?" Dee sounded hesitant and exhilarated at the same time.

"Yeah." He sucked her other nipple and looked up at her. "Remember, I'm the desperado. I intend to ravish you completely. Many times, *Señorita*."

Her eyes widened. "Oh, my."

"Kick off your shoes," he commanded. When she did, Jake tugged at her waistband. "Lift your hips." He yanked her slacks down and let them slide onto the ground.

Jake ground his teeth as he stared at the naked woman in his lap. It was almost more than he could handle. "Now spread your thighs."

Dee's lips parted as she obeyed, opening her pussy to him. "Okay."

"Say, *Sí, Señor*." Jake tried to sound gruff, like the desperado he was pretending to be.

Excitement flickered in her green eyes. "*Sí, Señor*."

Jake caressed the insides of her thighs, lightly brushing over the auburn curls, but not dipping into her. "Now, if you're a good *señorita*, I'll make you come."

"*Sí, Señor*." She nodded. "What do I have to do?"

He shifted in the saddle and continued stroking her skin in light circles. "Play with your nipples."

Moving her hand to her breast, Dee started to close her eyes.

"Keep your eyes open and look at me," Jake demanded. "Or I won't make you come."

"Yes…*Señor*."

Holding back a grin, he traced the curls, and then along her pussy lips. "Now beg me."

"Please." Dee swallowed and squirmed against his world class hard-on. "Please make me come, *Señor*."

He slipped his fingers into her heat, and thrust them deep inside. Dee arched her back against his arm at the same time she squeezed her nipple.

Jake moved his fingers up and stroked her clit, watching her face to see her expression when she reached her climax.

It was only a matter of seconds and Dee's body tensed and jerked as she came. The horse shifted beneath them, looked over his shoulder and snorted.

"Oh, God," Dee cried as she shuddered in his arms.

"You mean, oh, *Señor.*" Jake laughed and kissed her lips. "You know I'm not done having my way with you."

"Please, no." Dee's breathing was heavy as she stared up at him.

"Slide off the horse." Jake helped her sit up in his lap, and then eased her to the ground, careful not to scrape her soft skin over the saddle. "Don't move. Wait for me."

"*Sí, Señor.*" She stood a couple of feet away from the horse, her auburn hair flowing over her bare shoulders. Her hands were at her sides and she was completely naked except for her heart pendant.

Jake couldn't believe how much it turned him on to be playing out Dee's fantasy. He dismounted and then took the reins and loosely tied them to a tree. The gelding and mare both stood patiently, like the well-trained horses they were.

When he finished, he approached Dee. "If you're not a good *señorita*, I'll have to tie you up and fuck you against one of these trees."

"Tie me up?" Her hand moved to her throat, but he didn't think she was nervous. No, by the look in her eyes, he knew she was as excited as he.

"Yes." Jake kicked off his boots, and then went to the saddlebags and pulled out the blanket Dee had stored in one of the pockets. He laid the blanket out on the leaf and pine needle covered ground then stood. "Take off my pants, *Señorita*."

Dee approached him, almost shyly, undid the top button of his jeans and eased the zipper down. When she pulled down Jake's briefs, his cock sprung free. He sucked in his breath at the feel of the cool air against him.

She glanced up at him as he started to take off his Stetson, but she said, "No, leave it on. That's part of my fantasy. Please, *Señor*."

He held back a groan while she pushed down his briefs and jeans. She licked her lips as she knelt on the blanket, so close he could swear he felt her warm breath on his cock.

Jake kicked off his jeans and socks, and when Dee started to rise, he put his hand on her head. "Now pleasure me, *Señorita*."

A grin flashed across her face, but she quickly replaced it with a meek look. "*Sí, Señor*."

He caught his breath as she held his member in one hand and teased the head with her tongue. She licked and sucked him, lightly nibbling along his length as if he was a piece of corn on the cob. God, he'd never think of that vegetable the same way again.

"Take me deep in your throat," he commanded.

Dee answered by going down on him and taking him into her warm mouth. Jake groaned and slid his hands into her hair urging her on. She moved up and down his cock, twisting one hand around his cock as she sucked. Her other hand grabbed his hips, holding him close to her.

He gritted his teeth, knowing he was close to going over the edge. Dee's gaze met his while he watched himself go in and out of her mouth, and it shoved him over the chasm.

Jake shouted her name and clenched his hands in her hair. She held him to the back of her throat, moving her hand up and down, milking his semen and swallowing it.

Dee smiled and let him slide out of her mouth. She lifted her head and said, "How was that, *Señor*?"

"Fine." *Incredible. I could die a happy man.* Jake drew her up to him, letting his hands slide through her hair to her breasts. He pinched her nipple between his thumb and forefinger, and stared into her eyes. "But I'm not finished having my way with you, *Señorita*."

She trembled beneath his touch. "What do you want me to do next, *Señor*?"

"Feed me lunch. Naked."

Dee felt absolutely delicious, wearing nothing but her pendant as she took the saddlebag from her gelding and returned to the blanket Jake had laid out.

In real life she would never put up with a man ordering her around. But in acting out her fantasy, it was beyond fun. One of these days she would have to turn the tables on him and play dominatrix.

He looked so incredible, like a *Playgirl* centerfold with only his black cowboy hat and a seductive grin. And his cock was big and hard again.

While he settled on a boulder beside the blanket, Dee knelt beside Jake. He swallowed and forced himself to look at the horses instead of her naked body. Shadow lowered his head and munched grass. Whisper bent one knee, resting on her other three legs, looking like she was dozing off.

Jake turned back to see Dee withdrawing four sandwiches, two squares of fudge cake, and a thermos of iced tea, setting it all onto the blanket.

She held up two sandwiches. "Egg salad or roast beef?"

"Both." He eased onto the blanket and caught silken strands of her hair. Winding the strands around his finger, he played with them while she unwrapped their lunch. She started to hand him a sandwich, but he shook his head. "Feed it to me."

Smiling, she tore off a bite of the egg salad and held it to his lips. He opened his mouth and she fed it to him as his eyes held hers.

They fed each other one bite of sandwich at a time, a slow sensual meal like the one they'd had at the restaurant. Only this time they were alone. And naked.

With every movement Dee made, her breasts swayed. The smell of her sex called to him, making him want to taste her pussy, to devour her. By the time they were finished eating lunch, he was more than ready to bury his cock inside her.

She reached for the chocolate cake. "Dessert?"

"Uh-huh." Jake raked his gaze over her and heat pooled in his groin. "But I don't want cake."

"*Señor*?" She couldn't believe how it turned her on to call him that. "What would you prefer?"

"You." Jake grabbed his jeans and withdrew his leather belt. Holding his belt in one hand, he took Dee's hand in his other and brought her to her feet as he stood.

Dee raised an eyebrow. "Uh, you're not going to spank me with that, are you?"

Jake laughed. "No, I'm not into pain." He glanced around their hideaway and then led her to a young tree with fairly smooth bark. "Stand with your back to the tree, *Señorita*."

Her heart pounded faster as she realized he was going to carry out his earlier threat and tie her up like a desperado taking a young *señorita*. He brought her arms behind her and around the small tree trunk, then loosely bound them with his belt.

She could easily have pulled her hands away, but the feeling of being tied naked to a tree in their mountain hideaway was dangerous, exciting and exhilarating. With her hands bound behind her, her breasts jutted forward, her nipples hard and aching.

When Jake came back around, he frowned. "Is that bark too rough for your skin?"

"No." Dee shook her head and did her best to look meek. "What are you going to do to me, *Señor*?"

Desire flared in his eyes. "I intend to ravish you until you scream, my little *señorita*."

Dee licked her lips.

Jake put his hands on the tree above her head and stared down at her, his cock brushing against her belly. Dee quivered, dying for him to touch her.

He lightly nuzzled her hair, whispering endearments in Spanish, as though he was truly a Spanish lover. She breathed in the scent of their arousals as he caressed her ear with his warm breath, but still didn't touch her, other than his cock brushing her bare belly.

"*Besa me, por favor,*" Dee begged. "Kiss me, *Señor*."

Jake only brushed his lips lightly across hers. "You must please me if you want me to make you come again."

"Yes." Her body was on fire, and she trembled with the force of her need. "I'll do whatever you want."

He smiled and traced her mouth with the tip of his tongue. Dee parted her lips, but he didn't kiss her like she needed. Instead, he moved his mouth lower, lightly brushing the hollow of her throat. His hands were still above her, his body separated from hers, except for the occasional brushing of his cock. He was driving her out of her mind.

Jake pushed away from the tree and just looked at her for a moment.

"*Por favor, Señor.*" Dee arched her breasts toward him. "Fuck me, now."

He took off his hat and tossed it on a boulder to the side. Dee sighed as he grasped her hips and pressed himself against her, his cock hard against her belly.

Yes, that was what she needed.

No, she needed more.

Dee gasped as Jake captured her nipple in his mouth, lapping at it and then sucking it hard. He squeezed and kneaded her backside with his large hands, and started working his way down her belly with his lips.

Jake knelt in the leaves at her feet and pressed against the insides of her thighs with his fingers. "Spread your legs."

She widened her stance around his knees and then moaned as he slid a finger through the curls, and then between the folds of her pussy. She was so wet for him. She needed his mouth on her clit now.

He pressed his face into her curls and then slid his tongue against her nub.

"*Jake,*" Dee cried out, her hands straining against her bonds. She wanted to feel the silkiness of his hair as he devoured her, but it was so erotic being tied up by her desperado.

His tongue was warm and incredible as he lightly flicked it over her clit. He lifted his head and looked up at her. "Say, make me come again, *Señor.*"

"Please, God, yes." She could hardly talk, her breath was coming so hard and fast. "Make me come, *Señor.*"

Jake grinned and slid two fingers into her slick core. He bent his head and assaulted her pussy with his tongue, licking and sucking and lapping her clit as he thrust his fingers inside.

Dee felt as though her body was flying into a thousand pieces as she screamed and shuddered with her climax. Rainwater fell from the tree onto her hair as the tree shook with the strength of her orgasm.

After the last wave had subsided, Jake eased to his feet and kissed her long and hard. She tasted herself, mixed with his own unique flavor.

"Are you through ravishing me?" She asked when he lifted his head.

"Not on your life." Jake went behind the tree and untied the belt, freeing her hands. "Bring my hat, *Señorita*. I'm going to have my way with you some more."

Tingles skittered through Dee as she scooped up Jake's cowboy hat and handed it to him. "Your hat, *Señor*."

Jake pulled a condom from inside the hat rim then put on his Stetson, and she shivered with lust at the sight of him. So muscular, with his broad shoulders, narrow hips and powerful thighs.

"Come with me, *Señorita*." Taking Dee's hand, Jake led her to a high, flat boulder beside the stream that was still wet from the rain. After he arranged the blanket on its surface, he sat on the boulder and brought her between his knees. "I want you to ride me hard."

She nodded, mesmerized by his stormy gray eyes. "*Sí, Señor*."

"But first," he paused as he gave her a sinful grin, "suck my cock."

Dee smiled and knelt on the blanket. Holding him in one hand, she put her mouth over the head of his cock. Jake groaned as she slowly eased her mouth down and over him, flicking her tongue over him until he grabbed her head and forced her to stop.

Dee slid her mouth off him then looked at him from beneath her lashes. "Was that to your liking, *Señor*?"

"God, yes." Jake grinned and pulled her back up, then sheathed his cock. "Now straddle me."

With Jake's help, Dee climbed onto his lap and rubbed her pussy against his cock, aching to feel more of him. The blanket was cool beneath her knees and shins, but Jake's skin was hot.

She wiggled her hips and reached for his erection that was pressed against her belly. "I need you inside me."

Jake lifted his hat and put it on Dee's head, then put his hands on her hips. "Not yet. Your nipples are in the perfect spot for me to ravish."

He nuzzled and licked and sucked her breasts until she couldn't take it another moment, and begged him to enter her. "Now, Jake. Now!"

"Ride me hard. Real hard." He lifted her hips. Her scream of pleasure echoed through the small canyon as he thrust himself inside.

Dee grasped Jake's shoulders, digging her nails into his muscles and taking him deep. Not caring how hard the boulder was beneath the blanket, she bucked her hips at a frenzied pace, using the boulder as leverage to lift up and then go down again. Jake clenched her hips as she rode him.

Arching her back, Dee felt her hair slide against her naked shoulders, Jake's warm mouth on her breasts, his hands on her hips, and a cool breeze across her skin.

Her climax was so massive that she screamed louder than she ever had before. Jake shouted as he came, and Dee felt him pulsating deep within her.

She collapsed against him, and they held onto each other, their sweat mingling, their breathing heavy, their hearts pounding as one.

When Dee lifted her head, Jake's eyes met hers. "You're my kind of desperado," she murmured.

He laughed and pulled her close for a gentle kiss.

Sated by their lovemaking, Dee allowed herself to enjoy the comfort of Jake's embrace. His earthy presence surrounded her. Filled her.

The stream gurgled nearby and birds chattered in the trees. Goosebumps erupted over her body as a cool breeze brushed her bare skin.

Jake leaned back and traced one finger from her heart pendant to a hardened nipple. "Cold?"

"Not with you to warm me," Dee murmured in a teasing tone. The look in his eyes was too serious, and she was afraid he was going to say something she didn't want to hear.

Grasping a lock of her hair, he wrapped it around his hand. He took a deep breath, an uncertain look on his handsome face. "I need to know that you're ready to let me back into your heart."

God. He'd said it.

Dee shut her eyes to block him out.

Why couldn't he just have left it at sex and nothing more than that?

Then it hit her, and her stomach dropped.

She'd never stopped to consider Jake's feelings. All she'd been thinking about was herself.

"I—I've been so selfish," she whispered as she opened her eyes and met his stare. "I shouldn't have pushed you into…into a sexual relationship."

"What are you saying?" His voice was rough and the scar along his cheek grew whiter as his jaw tightened.

She wanted to look away from his steely gaze, but found she couldn't. "I don't have it in me to go through it again…someone I care about leaving me."

"I'm not going anywhere." He released his hold on her hair and rubbed his thumb along her jaw. "I'm staying right here."

Dee shook her head. "We can be friends, Jake. That's it. Just friends."

Chapter Thirteen

ဢ

After leaving Dee's, Jake had gone into his storage locker, dug out his weight training equipment and hauled everything back to his apartment. He set it all up smack in the middle of the living room, and then proceeded to lift weights until his muscles screamed.

They were still screaming a couple of hours later. He was going to pay for that workout. The whole time he'd pumped iron, he'd worked over in his mind Dee's insistence that they could only be friends.

Well, she could think that, but he was going to make sure they'd be more than friends and lovers. And sooner rather than later.

Jake splashed cold water over his face and neck, washing away some of the sweat, then grabbed a towel from the rack. Water streamed down his neck and onto his bare chest as he dried himself.

His thoughts turned to the rustling problem, and his concern for Dee. After seeing that intruder on her property, he didn't like the idea of her remaining on the ranch alone. It was a good two hundred yards from the bunkhouse to the ranch house, and if she screamed the ranch hands probably wouldn't even hear her.

As far as Jake was concerned, Dee wasn't going to be alone much longer.

He tossed the towel onto the pile of dirty clothes in his bathroom and headed to the kitchen. For dinner he fixed himself a peanut butter and grape jelly sandwich with a glass of cold milk to chase it down. The mood he was in, the sandwich tasted about as good as construction paper and rubber cement must taste.

While he ate, Jake couldn't help thinking about his incredible weekend with Dee.

Never in his wildest dreams had he imagined that she would go down on him in a restaurant, that they'd have sex outside in his truck cab, or that she would fulfill his dining room table fantasies by making herself come while he watched. Or that he would tie her to a tree and fuck her mindless.

Okay, in his wildest dreams he *had* imagined that kind of wild sex with Dee.

And he was harder than hell thinking about it.

Great sex aside, one thing had come through loud and clear this weekend—he was over his head in love with Dee. In truth, he knew he had never stopped loving her.

But this time he wasn't going to walk away. He wouldn't let anything chase him off—including Dee herself.

* * * * *

The day after she'd told Jake there couldn't be anything more than sex between them, Dee headed out to the barn. Almost mechanically, she brushed down and fed her horses Shadow and Whisper, and her sister Trace's old mare, Dancer.

When she finished, Dee stopped to check on the devil-eyed calf. Propping her arms on top of the stall door, she smiled at Imp, the little brat that had been such a challenge. But thanks to Jake, the calf was reasonably tame now.

A sad smile touched her lips as her thoughts turned to Jake, remembering that day he'd barreled into her barn wielding his gun, ready to defend her honor against Imp.

Jeez, was that less than a month ago? It seemed so much longer. Like he'd never left all those years ago.

Imp butted his head against the stall door, jarring Dee from her thoughts.

"Okay, son of Satan, I'll get your treat." She went to the big drum and scooped out a tin of the grain that smelled of oats and molasses, and poured it in the calf's trough.

"See you later, big guy," she murmured, stroking him on the nose as he ate. He really was the perfect calf. Each line, each curve — he'd make one hell of a stud some day.

Is that why someone loosened his latch? Dee backed away, surveying the stall. *Because he'll make fantastic breeding stock? Well, the hell with that. This little bastard is mine!*

With a sigh, Dee left the cool recesses of the barn and walked to the house, stuffing her work gloves in her jacket pocket. Overnight the weather had changed. The cool October day smelled of rain, and she wondered if they might be getting a fall storm.

She paused at the bottom of the porch steps to look off toward the mountain. What the hell was going on? It was like the mountain was opening up and swallowing her cattle whole.

Dee jogged up the steps and headed through the front door of the house. Her boots tapped against the tile as she strode to the kitchen, shedding her jacket as she went. Thoughts of her life and the paths she'd taken flashed through her mind.

And then it struck her.

Two paths. Two choices.

If she chose the first path, the path she was already on, she would remain alone.

If she gambled and chose the second, the future was less certain — but she might have a chance at happiness.

With the man she loved.

Oh, God.

Dee sank down in a chair at the kitchen table and buried her face in her hands.

She was in love with Jake. In truth, she knew she'd never stopped loving him, no matter how much she'd tried to deny it.

And Jake *had* changed. Over the past few weeks he'd been there for her every time she needed him. Especially when she didn't *think* she needed him, he'd been around anyway.

He'd promised to stay. This time he wasn't going to leave her.

The shrill ring of the telephone jolted her out of her thoughts.

Jake.

She snatched the cordless off the bedside table and punched the *on* button. Her voice was breathless as she answered. "Hello?"

"Hey, Dean. It's Catie."

The wave of disappointment that flooded Dee threw her off balance. She forced a bright note into her tone. "Hi, Catie."

"Are we still on for this evening?"

Dee frowned, trying to remember what she was supposed to be doing. "For what?"

"We're scheduled to bring over Shadow Warrior to service Whisper and Dancer, remember?"

Dee clapped her palm to her forehead. "Of course."

A man spoke to Catie, but Dee couldn't hear what he'd said.

Catie laughed. "Steve seems to think there was something in the deal about enchiladas for dinner, too."

"Enchiladas will be ready at five." Dee smiled. "Bring your appetites."

"Don't worry. I'll have Steve with me, so there won't be any leftovers."

After Dee said goodbye to Catie, she dialed Jake's number before she lost her nerve. She'd invite him over to have dinner with them, and then she'd get him alone and tell him.

I love you.

Her hands trembled and her heart fluttered as the phone rang. And rang.

Jake's answering machine didn't even pick up. Disappointment ebbed through her as she hung up and went to get dinner ready for the Wilds. She'd just have to try to get a hold of Jake later.

* * * * *

"Well?" Catie picked up the salad bowl in one hand and two bottles of dressing in the other as she helped Dee set the table. "Is Jake still a good fuck?"

Heat rushed to Dee's cheeks as she pulled the oven door open to retrieve the enchiladas, but it wasn't the heat from the oven warming her face. She grabbed a pair of potholders, withdrew the pan and set it on the counter, closing the oven door with her hip.

Dee met her friend's expectant gaze and laughed. "Oh, my God, is he ever."

"You *go*, girl." Catie's short blonde hair bounced as she grinned and carried the salad and dressing into the dining room.

Dee opened the fridge and searched for the hot sauce, sour cream and guacamole. When she had gathered the items, she grabbed the bag of blue corn chips off the counter and took everything to the dining table.

The slamming of the front door and male voice alerted Dee to the approach of Jess and Catie's brother, Steve.

"I invited Lawless to join us if you don't mind," Steve said as they entered the dining room.

Catie gave Jess a sexy grin. "*I* sure don't mind."

"Plenty to go around." Dee gestured toward the table. "You three go ahead and sit down and I'll grab the enchiladas."

Dee dodged into the kitchen, then returned with the casserole dish and placed it at the center of the table. The spicy scent filled the dining room as she spooned generous helpings of enchiladas onto everyone's plate and added servings of crisp salad along with it.

When her friends were taken care of, Dee took her seat and they dug into the meal. Laughter and chatter went on through dinner, Catie openly flirting with Jess. By the glint in his wicked blue eyes, the foreman seemed to enjoy Catie's attraction, although he made no move to pursue it.

Dee only wished that Jake could have been there to enjoy the dinner with her friends. She could barely focus on the conversation around her. All she wanted was to be with Jake.

"These enchiladas are terrific," Jess said as he took a second helping.

"Thanks." Dee spooned a pool of salsa onto her plate and added a few corn chips next to it. "Mexican food is my favorite thing to make and eat."

"Not me." Catie reached for the sour cream. "I like it, but my fave is anything Italian."

Cool liquid slid down Dee's throat as she took a sip of iced tea. She set the glass down and turned to Steve. "Did you lose any cattle when your fence was cut?"

Steve nodded. "A few, but nothing like you or Kev Grand." He looked at Jess. "Heard Deputy Forrester stopped by. Any word from him? Are they close to catching these damn rustlers?"

"He came by yesterday, while Dee was off with Reynolds." Jess shook his head. "Either Forrester doesn't know anything about what's going on, or he's not saying. The man's real hard to read."

"So what's next?" Catie asked, her dark brown eyes focused on Jess.

A hard look came over Jess's handsome features. "Clues are adding up. We'll catch the bastards."

"How's everything with you?" Dee asked Steve as she dunked a chip into the salsa on her plate.

He shrugged and took a drink of iced tea. "About as good as always." Steve set his glass down and picked up his fork. "The other day I ran into Jake Reynolds. Looks like he's been offered a big promotion for the work he's done. I've heard around town that he's one of the best agents that Customs has."

A warm rush of pleasure went through Dee as she heard about Jake's success.

Steve stuck his fork into his enchiladas. "Too bad he has to transfer to California to accept the promotion, though."

Dee's smile froze and she felt blood draining through her body to her toes. "Oh," she managed to say before lowering her gaze and dropping the tortilla chip onto her plate.

Her head buzzed and she was painfully aware of Catie's silence.

The truth struck Dee like a storm. She'd told Jake she didn't want anything past sex. And now, Jake was leaving.

Again.

And she had done the unthinkable. She had fallen in love with him.

Again.

Her devastation was complete. Dee had never felt so furious and so miserable at the same time — except for the last time Jake left her.

"Honey, are you okay?" Catie's voice seemed distant, like she was talking from some other planet.

The room went deadly quiet as Dee struggled to control her emotions. To keep her face from revealing how badly she'd been crushed.

"I'm fine." She glanced up from her plate and forced her smile to unfreeze. The men looked uncomfortable and started eating their enchiladas again, the only sounds the scrape of forks against plates.

A deep male voice shattered the silence, "I hope I'm not interrupting anything."

Dee snapped her head up. A thrill shot through her when she saw Jake towering over her. But his jaw was clenched, his eyes stormy gray.

Words froze in her throat and she couldn't move.

He'd come to tell her goodbye.

But hell if she was going to let him.

Jake gave the Wilds' and Jess each a quick nod. "If you'll excuse us, Dee and I need to talk." And then he moved so fast that Dee didn't have time to react. She yelped as he grabbed her around the waist, and then her world spun as he flung her over his shoulder.

"Jake!" Blood rushed to her head as she struggled against his hold. "What do you think you're doing?"

"What I should have done ten years ago." He wrapped his arms tighter around Dee's thighs and backside, trying to control the struggling woman over his shoulder.

He looked at Dee's amused friends. "You all finish up here," Jake said. "Dee won't be back for a good long while."

Catie smiled and gave him the thumbs up. "We'll be fine."

"Well, what're you waiting for?" Jess said, waving toward the front door, and Catie laughed.

Jake grinned and turned on his heel and marched out the door.

Dee pounded on his back as he closed the door behind them. "You're going to regret this."

"Then I guess I'd better not let you go." Jake jogged down the steps to his truck, intentionally letting his hands slide under her skirt now that they didn't have an audience.

God, this desperado stuff turned him on.

"Don't do that," she said, but her demand came out in a low moan.

He chuckled. "I seem to remember this being your fantasy."

"That'll teach me to tell you my secrets." If he wasn't mistaken, Dee was laughing. "Now put me down."

When he stopped in front of the passenger door of his truck, he shifted so that Dee's legs parted. He slid his fingers between her thighs, felt her damp panties and grinned. She was just as turned on as he was.

"*Don't.*" Dee's voice wavered. "Stop."

"Don't stop?" he teased.

"You know what I mean."

"I know what you're saying, but your body is telling me something else altogether, sweetheart."

"You're impossible!"

Jake opened the truck door, slid her off his shoulder and plopped her onto the front seat. "We're going to have ourselves a little talk."

"You better believe it." Folding her arms, Dee glared at Jake, but he saw passion burning in her eyes. He almost groaned out loud at the sight of her denim skirt hiked up her thighs and her silky red panties peeking beneath it.

After he shut the door, he went around to the driver's side and climbed in. He stuffed the keys in the ignition, started the truck and backed out of the driveway.

Dee turned and faced him, her head tilted. "So, where are you taking me?"

Jake guided his vehicle down the dirt road, waiting a moment before answering her question. "I'd intended to take you out to a restaurant, but looks like we're going to need someplace a little more private."

Because he wasn't going to be able to wait much longer before he had to fuck her.

Like now. At the side of the road. In broad daylight. In his truck cab.

"Really?" She scooted next to him and slid her hand along his thigh. "That's good, because I've got a—" Her hand caressed his cock. "—bone to pick with you."

He gritted his teeth and forced himself to keep his eyes on the road as she continued to stroke his cock through his jeans. "Ah, Dee. You'd better ease up."

A low laugh spilled from her lips, but she refused to stop. When Jake had parked the truck in front of his apartment, he dragged her out of the truck with him. He couldn't unlock the door to the apartment fast enough to get her alone.

"What's this?" She eyed the weight training equipment that filled the living room. "You turned your home into a gymnasium?"

He let the door slam shut behind him. "Something like that."

Jake gripped Dee by the shoulders and spun her around. Her eyes widened and her lips parted, but before she had a chance to say a word, he crushed his mouth to hers, hard and demanding. She returned his kiss just as frantically.

He grabbed her hips and pressed her firmly against his cock. They ravished each other's mouths, an incredibly wild kiss. He shoved her blouse and bra up and over her breasts, and she moaned as he covered them with his palms.

"I need you," he groaned, tweaking and plucking her nipples.

"Oh, God." Dee's hands shook as she undid his belt, then the top button of his pants. She yanked down the zipper and then his briefs, and gave a triumphant cry when his enormous cock spilled into her palms.

He released her breasts to grab her skirt and pull it up around her waist. He pushed down the bikini underwear, and in a quick movement she stepped out of them.

Jake spun her and pressed her against the wall. "Clamp your legs around my waist and hold on."

"Hurry," she moaned as she complied, crossing her ankles behind him and wrapping her arms around his neck.

Jake slid on protection and then Dee cried out as he plunged his cock into her slick core. Again and again he thrust into her as she clung to him, their mouths mating even as their bodies were.

He was so close, so close to going over the edge. He wanted to take her with him, but he didn't know if he could hold off much longer.

In the next instant, Dee went rigid in his arms, vibrating with her orgasm, taking Jake over the summit along with her. While his climax shuddered through him, he slumped against Dee, her arms around his neck, his chest against hers. For a moment neither said a word, and he felt their hearts pounding in rhythm to their heavy breathing. Her orange blossom scent, and the smells of their passion filled his senses.

Keeping Dee pressed tight against him, he carried her down the hall.

"Wow. Do you ever know how to show a girl a good time." She clung to his neck and leaned back to give him a satisfied smile. "You can be my desperado any day."

Jake felt his cock hardening again. God, he couldn't get enough of this woman. When he reached the small bedroom, he all but tossed her on the full-sized bed.

Eyes wide, Dee propped herself on her elbows, her skirt hiked up around her waist, her blouse and bra above her breasts, and her sandals still on. Her auburn hair was in a wild tangle around her face, her lips swollen and cheeks flushed.

And she was wearing the heart pendant he'd given her.

His chest constricted and his throat closed off. He wasn't about to let her go this time. He couldn't.

Dee tried to catch her breath as she stared up at Jake. She was incredibly turned on. Again.

For countless seconds he stood over her, as though assessing what step to take next. His black hair was mussed, his face unshaven, his masculine body large and imposing, his gray eyes dark and stormy.

Slowly he removed his shirt and tossed it onto the nightstand. He shed the rest of his clothing, his eyes fixed on her, until he was completely naked. His cock jutted out and she longed to touch it, to touch all of him.

Her heart pounded in her throat as Jake knelt and took her sandals off her feet. Carefully he undressed her, until all she was only wearing was the peridot heart, and then he eased her to the center of the bed and lay down beside her.

It seemed like an eternity passed as he stroked her hair from her face, his touch gentle. Warm and caring and…loving.

He leaned over her, their eyes locked, and then he kissed her. His lips moved over hers, so tender and sweet that tears came to her eyes.

Jake pulled away and studied her. "What's wrong?" he asked softly, cupping her jaw and brushing a tear away with his thumb. His fingers felt calloused and warm against her skin.

"My cowboy prince." Dee caressed the scar along his cheek, his stubble like sandpaper to her palm. "You're not leaving me behind."

He stilled. "What?"

"Steve Wilds told me about the promotion." She moved both arms around his neck. "I'm sorry, baby, but you're not getting rid of me that easy. If you're going to California, you're going to have company. Permanently."

The tension easing from his face and body was visible. "It's a good thing. If I had to carry you over my shoulder to the altar, I would do it."

Dee smiled. "You weren't planning on leaving?"

"Ah, sweetheart." His eyes told her the depth of his feelings. "I realized that ten years ago I'd made the biggest mistake of my life. I could never leave you again."

Warmth crept through Dee, her body tingling from head to toe. "Damn straight."

Jake laughed and rolled over to grab his shirt off the nightstand. He stuck his hand in the breast pocket, and brought it back out, something clenched in his fist. He let the shirt slide to the floor as his gaze met hers and said, "Close your eyes, Cinderella."

Tremors ran through Dee as she lowered her eyelids. Jake took her left hand and slid a metal band onto her finger. "You can look now."

Her hand trembled as she opened her eyes and saw the diamond ring, the marquis stone glittering in the light. And on each side of the diamond, a peridot was set in the gold band.

Jake's gray eyes focused intently on her. "I love you, Dee. I've never stopped loving you. Say you'll marry me and I'll do whatever I can to make up for all the time we've lost."

"You bastard." She flung her arms around his neck and buried her face against his chest. "I love you so much."

He pulled away from her and grinned. "Is that a yes?"

"A most definite yes." Dee cradled his jaw in her palm. "And I'm not waiting another minute. We can fly to Vegas tomorrow. I don't want to give you a chance to change your mind."

"There's no danger of that." He kissed her long and slow, then murmured, "Why wait that long? We can catch a flight tonight."

"I'll hold you to that." She was so full of love and happiness that she thought she'd explode. "We'll start packing, just as soon as you finish fucking me again."

He smiled and slid between her thighs. "I love you, Dee MacLeod."

She grabbed his cock and slid him inside her pussy, giving him her orneriest grin. "You'd better, Jake Reynolds. You'd better."

Epilogue

ೞ

Catie Wilds pulled at her earlobe as she guided her battered ranch pickup into the parking lot of the Cochise County Sheriff's Department. She'd had it up to *here* with the damn cattle rustling, and she was determined to give the sheriff a piece of her mind.

After she parked, she stormed out of the pickup, slamming the door behind her. Catie had been pissed about Dean MacLeod's cattle being stolen, but now that the Wilds Ranch had been ripped off, it was definitely *personal.*

Shoving the glass doors open, Catie stomped into the reception area.

A busty brunette raised a sculpted eyebrow, her scarlet lips set in a what-the-hell-do-you-want smile. "May I help you?"

"I'd like to see Sheriff Savage." Catie propped her hands on her slim jean-clad hips. "Now."

"I don't think he's available." Boob Queen gave a don't-you-wish-he-was-available sniff as she picked up the phone. "Let me check."

Her temper escalating beyond eruption level, Catie glanced past the reception area. She looked into a room that was empty save for desks sporting computers and equipment...and that sorry excuse for a deputy, Ryan Forrester.

Without so much as a by-your-leave, Catie turned on her booted heel and headed straight for Forrester. She set her gaze on stun with shoot-to-kill as an alternative if the deputy didn't give her satisfaction.

"You can't…" Miss Mega-Tits spouted behind Catie.

"I need a word with you." Catie strode right up to Ryan, propped her hands on her hips, and frowned up at him. At only five foot four, she only came up to the deputy's shoulder — but her glare was enough to cut down a man three times her size. And Catie knew how to wield her icy gaze like a sword.

Ryan's Adam's apple bobbed and he diverted his eyes, waving off Boob Woman, then turned his attention back to Catie. "What do you need, Cat?"

"I'll *tell* you what I need." Catie poked one finger at his chest, punctuating each word with a jab at his shirt. "I need my goddamned heifers back. I need you guys to get off your asses and figure out who the hell is stealing everyone's cattle."

Forrester stepped back. "We're working on it."

"Don't give me that crap." Catie advanced on the deputy as he retreated. "Get me the sheriff. *Now.*"

"What can I do for you?" A deep rumbling voice startled Catie out of her tirade and shivers shot down her spine.

She whipped her head to the side and her gaze locked with the most amazing crystalline green eyes — and the hottest man she'd ever seen. Her panties grew damp, every coherent thought fleeing her mind as she got lost in the pull of those magnetic eyes.

He had his hip and shoulder propped against the doorway of an office, his thumbs hooked in the pockets of his snug Wranglers. The man raised one hand to push up the brim of his tan felt Stetson as he studied her. His sable mustache twitched as he smiled, causing Catie's small nipples to harden into tiny torpedoes pointed straight at him.

Oh. My. God. For the first time in her life, Catie Wilds was speechless.

Sheriff Jarrod Savage studied the little wildcat who'd stormed into his office and had been in the middle of ripping Deputy Forrester a new one. Damn she'd been cute as she'd spouted off at Forrester. Jarrod had enjoyed watching the flush in her fair cheeks, how her short blonde hair shimmered as she spoke and the way that sprinkling of freckles made her look so damn adorable.

He'd almost hated to interrupt her. And now…*well, hell.* The desire that sparked in those chocolate brown eyes charged up his own libido and it'd be a wonder if no one noticed the hardening in his cock. Something in his gut told him this was a woman worth getting to know—in every way a man could know a woman.

He pushed away from the door of his office and strode toward her. "Jarrod Savage," he said as he held out his hand.

Forrester mumbled something about "work to be done," and headed on out of the office, leaving Jarrod alone with the woman in the empty control room.

"Catie Wilds." The petite woman drew herself up and raised her chin as she took his hand.

Her vanilla musk teased his senses, along with the current sizzling between them as he took her hand in his. He wished he wasn't on duty so he could make things a little more personal between them. "A most definite pleasure, Catie Wilds."

As though remembering why she was there in the first place, the little spitfire pulled her hand from his and stepped back. "This cattle rustling bullshit has gone on long enough."

Jarrod nodded as he hooked his thumbs in his pockets. "You're telling me."

"Well what do you intend to do about it?" Catie propped her hands on her hips, that fiery glint back in her eyes. "We just lost fifteen heifers last night. We're one of the smaller ranches in the area, and that's something we sure as hell can't afford."

Frustration at their inability to track the bastards down was a fire in Jarrod's gut. "Believe me, we're putting everything and everyone we can on it."

"Obviously that's not good enough." Catie raised her chin. "What's it been? Six weeks since this whole mess started?"

Jarrod ran a hand over his mustache. "I know it's not what you want to hear, but we're working on it."

"Well that's just *great*." The little wildcat spun on her heel and marched out of the control room.

He had to hold back a smile as he watched the natural sway of her slim hips as she headed out the front door, muttering something about, "Damn bureaucrats."

Jarrod shifted his position, trying to alleviate the new ache in his cock.

Looked like he'd have to pay a visit to the Wilds Ranch.

About the Author

Cheyenne McCray is the award-winning author of sixteen books and six novellas. Among other accolades, Chey has been presented with the prestigious Romantic Times BOOKclub's Reviewers' Choice Award for "Best Erotic Romance of the Year".

Chey has been writing ever since she can remember, back to her kindergarten days when she penned her first poem. She always knew one day she would write novels, hoping her readers would get lost in the worlds she created, as she did when she was lost in a good book. Cheyenne enjoys spending time with her husband and three sons, traveling, and of course writing, writing, writing.

Cheyenne welcomes comments from readers. You can find her website and email address on her author bio page at www.ellorascave.com.

Enjoy An Excerpt From
Wildcat

Book 2 in the Wild series

Copyright © Cheyenne McCray, 2003.

Chapter One

ॐ

Catie Wilds checked the grandfather clock in the hallway and smiled. It was almost time for her *rendezvous*. Just the thought of what she was about to do made her feel naughty and absolutely delicious inside.

Wood floorboards creaked under her bare feet as she hurried to her bedroom. The old ranch house smelled of dust, lemon oil, and the single-serving lasagna she'd nuked in the microwave earlier. Unlike the modern MacLeod ranch house, Catie's home was well over a century old and looked every bit of it. But it was home.

When she reached her room, she closed the door in case her older brother Steve happened to come home early. The two had been running the ranch together since their father and his wife—number six—had been killed in a car accident, some five years ago.

And of course they hadn't seen their "real" mother since they were in elementary school. The woman had run off with a muscle-bound Mr. Arizona. Apparently that fling hadn't lasted, but good old "Mom" had enjoyed her freedom too much to get around to coming back home.

Catie pulled her pocketknife out and tossed it on her chest of drawers. She shimmied out of her jeans, her thoughts turning to the only person who'd even been close to being like a mom to her. Mrs. Karchner, who'd given Catie that pocketknife, used to own the ranch down the road from the Wilds. Mrs. Karchner had been the one stable person in Catie's wild youth. But the woman passed away a few years ago, breaking Catie's heart.

She sighed as she yanked her T-shirt over her head and tossed it onto the bed. She sure missed that woman.

After growing up in a broken family and witnessing too many failed marriages, Catie didn't believe in commitment. But she sure as hell believed in having as much fun as possible with the opposite sex.

Maybe she was too much like her mother.

Forcing the thoughts from her mind, Catie removed her bra and thong underwear and then pulled on a tiny jean skirt and a button-up blouse. She loved the feeling of being naked beneath her clothes, and it would make tonight's experience all the more fun. The jean material of her skirt felt rough and sexy against her bare skin and caused her pussy to throb and ache.

And since meeting the sexy new county sheriff yesterday, she'd been horny as all get out. Too bad she'd been pissed about the stolen cattle when she met that sex god of a cowboy. Or she'd have been tempted to jump the man. Well, for now she was putting aside any thought of rustling, money woes, and lack of a man with a good cock. She had a show to catch.

Once she had put on her leather moccasins, Catie slipped into the moonlit night that smelled crisp and clean from the rains of the past couple of days. Her nipples puckered and her heart beat a little faster as she picked her way through the tumbleweeds and mesquite bushes, out toward the cabin at the back of the ranch. Her moccasins made no sound as she stole along the slightly muddy path as quickly as she could.

She wanted to get there in time to watch *everything*.

And from the conversation she'd overheard this morning between Brad Taylor and the Wilson twins, there was going to be plenty to watch.

Catie had never spied on people having sex before, and she couldn't believe how turned-on she was just thinking about watching the three of them go at it. Well, there was that time she'd caught Dean MacLeod masturbating, and that had been erotic to watch from her hiding place in Dean's kitchen—and it had certainly whet her appetite for enjoying another bout of voyeurism.

Tumbleweeds scraped Catie's bare legs and an Arizona October breeze found its way underneath her mini skirt, straight to her bare pussy. It felt cool and erotic, and she was already incredibly wet. The sense of danger, coupled with the possibility of getting caught spying on one of the ranch hands in ménage à trois, heightened her excitement.

Catie had loved to play in the old cabin when she was a kid, and had kept the place in decent shape over the years as a kind of getaway when she wanted some time alone. When Brad had asked to use the cabin, she'd thought nothing of it—until she'd overheard his conversation with Sabrina and Sasha Wilson.

Even as Catie skirted the cabin to the back, she saw Brad's truck parked outside and heard feminine laughter from within. Damn, but she hoped she hadn't missed any of the good stuff.

She eased up to the back wall of the cabin, to a knothole that was just low enough that she had to bend over. Her skirt hiked up over her ass cheeks, and she felt the breeze on her pussy again as she peeked through the hole.

And got an eyeful.

* * * * *

Voices floated through the night air and Spirit's ears pricked toward the sound. Jarrod Savage brought the mare to a halt, and after listening for a moment, he swung down and let the reins drop to the ground. The mare was well-trained and intelligent, and wouldn't move unless Jarrod whistled to her.

Once he checked his utility belt and his firearm, Jarrod holstered the gun and quietly headed toward the sounds that were coming from a small cabin he could just make out in the moonlight.

For the past few weeks, despite what one Miss Catie Wilds might think, he'd been investigating a rash of cattle rustling that had escalated in this part of the state. As the new county sheriff, Jarrod's reputation was riding on getting this case solved, and getting it solved *now.*

He eased through the dry grass and tumbleweeds, his hand resting on his weapon's grip, his senses on high alert, on the lookout for the slightest indication of danger.

The flash of white caught Jarrod's eye and he froze. His eyes narrowed as he watched the small figure stealing through the night, to the back of the cabin. When the figure moved up to the wall, light from inside the cabin shone on her face.

A woman. A damn beautiful…and a familiar woman at that.

Jarrod grinned as he realized it was that little spitfire of a rancher who'd come storming into his office yesterday. Catie Wilds had more than peaked his interest. His cock had been on full-throb every time he'd thought about her since.

And as she bent over to peek into a hole in the wall of the cabin, Catie's short blonde hair swung forward. Her next-to-nothing-skirt hiked up — the moonlight illuminating her completely naked ass and pussy.

Despite years of law enforcement training and plenty of practice in keeping emotionally and physically detached from his work, Jarrod couldn't help but feel a stirring in his cock. He swallowed, hard, as Catie licked her lips and began fondling her breasts while she looked through the hole, into the cabin.

Feminine laughter came from inside the cabin, and then a woman's voice said, "Lick my pussy, Brad."

Jarrod's mouth turned up into a grin. The perky little blonde was a dang Peeping Tom. Or rather a Peeping Tomasina.

His cock grew even harder as he watched her move one hand beneath her skirt while her other hand continued to pluck one nipple through her blouse...

East of Easy

By Linda Bleser

Kate Feathers had it all. As representative of her hometown of Easy in the Miss Arizona State Pageant, the future held unlimited possibilities. Then it all came crashing down. The victim of malicious rumors, Kate was stripped of her crown, her scholarship and her future. She left town in shame, running as far east of Easy as possible.

Ten years later, Kate returns home to settle her mother's estate. She thought she was immune to the small-town gossip she'd left behind, but an unexpected meeting with Max Connors, the high-school sweetheart she blames for starting the ugly rumors, uncovers secrets and lies that are as painful now as they were then.

Kate simply wants to get her mother's affairs in order so she can return to New York, but her growing attraction to Max — and a series of inscrutable messages from a haunted teacup — will force her to face her worst fears once and for all.

And this time, running is not an option.

Later that evening, Kate sat alone in her mother's kitchen. She'd managed to hold herself together as long as she'd kept busy, but with the last hushed goodbye from well-meaning visitors, grief crept in and filled the silence.

The house had changed little. Looking around the familiar kitchen, the years slipped away. She'd known coming home would bring back memories. She'd shored herself up, prepared for the worst. Ten years was a long time, but so much had changed. She'd grown up. Matured. She could deal with a few bad memories.

But she hadn't been prepared for the unexpected rush of *sweet* memories—doing homework at the cracked Formica table while Lillian made grilled-cheese sandwiches on the stove, or sneaking a cookie from the ceramic cookie jar while Lillian chatted on the phone and Jeff built Lego cities on the floor. Those remembrances of happier times hurt almost as much as the more painful ones she'd nurtured over the years. They only reminded her of how much she'd lost.

Walking through the house, Kate focused on the little changes—the new lace curtains replacing the yellow dotted Swiss she remembered, the wrought-iron baker's rack in the corner draped with pottery and fresh ivy, a teapot-shaped clock over the window. Each small change pierced her heart with a fresh wave of remorse. Life had gone on here while she'd held it unchanged in her memory. Little by little, Lillian had given up waiting for her daughter to come home.

Home. Kate had thought it would always be here waiting for her. Now that she was back, she wondered why she'd waited so long. How many times had Lillian begged her to come home for a visit? The years had slipped by while Kate had made one excuse after another, too afraid to face the small-town gossip that had sent her running in the first place.

Pushing the negative thoughts aside, Kate busied herself around the kitchen, feeling like an intruder as she opened drawers and cabinets. She tucked the last covered casserole into the freezer, wrapped the cookies and desserts dropped off by neighbors, wiped the counter, then went through the house turning lights on. It was too dark, too quiet.

Her overnight bag rested against the sofa where she'd left it that morning. It seemed so long ago. She hadn't had a moment to herself since she'd arrived, and now that she was alone, the silence felt suffocating. She carried the suitcase into her old bedroom and placed it on the familiar lace-edged comforter. Matching curtains fluttered in the window. Nothing had changed in this room. The linens were crisp and fresh in anticipation of her arrival, and the scent of lemon polish hung in the air. It was almost as if she'd never left.

She unzipped her bag and unpacked the few things she'd brought along. She'd only intended to stay the weekend and realized she'd have to pick up a few things now that her plans had changed. Maybe she'd drive into Phoenix during the week and do some shopping.

The doorbell jangled, interrupting her thoughts. Kate clutched a folded pair of jeans to her chest. Who could that be? She didn't think she could stand another neighbor dropping by to offer condolences. She stood very still, hoping whoever it was would go away. Another buzz convinced her otherwise. She sighed and dropped the jeans onto the bed.

Kate trudged to the door. Every ounce of strength seemed to have been drained from her body, leaving her limp. With a sigh, she opened the front door then blinked in surprise. Standing on the porch step was a boy of eight or nine with tousled sun-bleached hair and tear-stained cheeks. He held up a handful of sagging wildflowers.

"These are for Miz Lilly," he said in a trembling voice. "To take up to heaven."

Kate knelt down on one knee and took the flowers. Only then did she notice the aluminum forearm crutches and metal braces strapped around his legs. "Thank you," she said, feeling her own lip quiver. "What's your name?"

"Bobby," he replied, brushing a fist across tear-smudged cheeks. His shoulders hitched on a quiet sob.

Kate fought the urge to brush her fingers through the boy's tousled hair. She clutched the wilting wildflowers to her chest. Of all the lavish displays that had filled the funeral parlor, this fistful of hand-picked flowers from a child was the most precious.

The boy turned and walked away, the braces on his legs giving him a slow, side-to-side gait. Kate noticed the red pick-up truck idling by the side of the road.

Max?

She couldn't be sure. It was too dark to see inside the truck. Besides, half the male population of Easy drove pick-ups.

Her heart lurched at the thought of seeing Max again. That, more than anything else, convinced Kate it was too dangerous to stay in Easy for long. She couldn't let Max Connors worm his way into her heart again. She'd spent too many years trying to forget, too many lonely nights crying into her pillow for a love that was lost and a trust betrayed. Max was her past. He'd never be her future.

The little boy stopped before reaching the truck and turned back to Kate. "Miz Lilly was my friend," he said, his lips turned down in a brave struggle to keep from crying. "I'll miss her."

"So will I," Kate admitted, watching as the boy made his way to the road and climbed into the passenger's side of the truck. She turned and walked inside, then leaned against the closed door. "So will I."

The boy's simple gesture broke down the control she'd struggled so hard to maintain. She slid to the floor, clutching the flowers to her chest and rocking like a child. How could she have let so much time go by? Who was she really punishing by not coming home all these years?

Her chest heaved and tears of loss and regret flowed unchecked. She'd thought her mother would always be here, that home was a place to which she could always return. Now nothing would ever be the same again.

Sobs clawed her throat raw and she cried until she couldn't cry anymore.

Why an electronic book?

We live in the Information Age—an exciting time in the history of human civilization, in which technology rules supreme and continues to progress in leaps and bounds every minute of every day. For a multitude of reasons, more and more avid literary fans are opting to purchase e-books instead of paper books. The question from those not yet initiated into the world of electronic reading is simply: *Why?*

1. *Price.* An electronic title at Ellora's Cave Publishing and Cerridwen Press runs anywhere from 40% to 75% less than the cover price of the exact same title in paperback format. Why? Basic mathematics and cost. It is less expensive to publish an e-book (no paper and printing, no warehousing and shipping) than it is to publish a paperback, so the savings are passed along to the consumer.

2. *Space.* Running out of room in your house for your books? That is one worry you will never have with electronic books. For a low one-time cost, you can purchase a handheld device specifically designed for e-reading. Many e-readers have large, convenient screens for viewing. Better yet, hundreds of titles can be stored within your new library—on a single microchip. There are a variety of e-readers from different manufacturers. You can also read e-books on your PC or laptop computer. (Please note that Ellora's Cave does not endorse any specific brands. You can check our websites at www.ellorascave.com or

www.cerridwenpress.com for information we make available to new consumers.)

3. ***Mobility.*** Because your new e-library consists of only a microchip within a small, easily transportable e-reader, your entire cache of books can be taken with you wherever you go.

4. ***Personal Viewing Preferences.*** Are the words you are currently reading too small? Too large? Too… ANNOYING? Paperback books cannot be modified according to personal preferences, but e-books can.

5. ***Instant Gratification.*** Is it the middle of the night and all the bookstores near you are closed? Are you tired of waiting days, sometimes weeks, for bookstores to ship the novels you bought? Ellora's Cave Publishing sells instantaneous downloads twenty-four hours a day, seven days a week, every day of the year. Our webstore is never closed. Our e-book delivery system is 100% automated, meaning your order is filled as soon as you pay for it.

Those are a few of the top reasons why electronic books are replacing paperbacks for many avid readers.

As always, Ellora's Cave and Cerridwen Press welcome your questions and comments. We invite you to email us at Comments@ellorascave.com or write to us directly at Ellora's Cave Publishing Inc., 1056 Home Avenue, Akron, OH 44310-3502.

THE
✞ ELLORA'S CAVE ✞
LIBRARY

Stay up to date with Ellora's Cave Titles in
Print with our Quarterly Catalog.

TO RECIEVE A CATALOG,
SEND AN EMAIL WITH YOUR NAME
AND MAILING ADDRESS TO:

CATALOG@ELLORASCAVE.COM

OR SEND A LETTER OR POSTCARD
WITH YOUR MAILING ADDRESS TO:

CATALOG REQUEST
c/o ELLORA'S CAVE PUBLISHING, INC.
1056 HOME AVENUE
AKRON, OHIO 44310-3502

Make each day more *EXCITING* With our

ELLORA'S CAVEMEN

CALENDAR

COMING TO A BOOKSTORE NEAR YOU!

ELLORA'S CAVE

Bestselling Authors Tour